I0681292

The Burzee Rose

A Christmas Carol

Also by Alan Lindsay (alanglindsay.com)
A. a novel
Ambaguam, Beginning at the End

With Dennis Anfuso (dennisanfuso.com)
OzHouse
OzHouse Reopened, The Curse of Budistiltskin

THE

BURZEE

ROSE

A

CHRISTMAS

CAROL

Interset Press

2017

The Burzee Rose, A Christmas Carol by Alan Lindsay
Copyright © 2017 by Alan Lindsay
All rights reserved. No part of this book may be reproduced or transmitted in any form or by any means, electronic or mechanical, including photocopying, recording, scanning, or by any information storage and retrieval system, including the Internet and the World Wide Web, without permission from the Publisher, except in the case of brief quotations embodied in critical articles and reviews. This is a work of fiction. Any resemblance of characters in this book to actual persons living or dead is unintentional and purely coincidental. Honest.
9 8 7 6 5 4 3 2 1 /0 1
Interset Press
35 Burns Hill Road
Wilton, New Hampshire 03086
Interset Press is a registered trademark and "Fiddler," the Interset Press colophon, is a trademark of Linda Anfuso.

Printed in the United States of America.
First Interset Press edition: May 2017.
Library of Congress Cataloguing-in-Publication Data:
        Lindsay, Alan
Cover art by Dan Fuso
Book design by Guy Ravin
Title: **The Burzee Rose, A Christmas Carol**
Summary: Morris' life would have been great—if not for his new stepsisters and those crazy little men who thought they were elves. No matter. Morris's latest stepmother would certainly be gone by Christmas like all the rest. Wasn't she already trolling on the internet all day for her next husband? But would she take Jasmine and Tanya with her? And why did these girls want to pull him into their troubles anyway? He just wanted to play video games. Everything with have blown over if that substation hadn't blown up. But when the power blew and he scurried out to get gas for the generator, Jasmine just had to go with him. And then they stumbled into those reindeer and that rogue pair of little men on a mission to rescue the North Pole. And then—wouldn't you know it—they had to get themselves sucked into the time vortex. So now there were two problems to solve: Claire and Christmas.
[1. Fantasy. 2. Mystery. 3. Christmas 4. Burzee. 5. Lindsay, Alan.] 1. Title [Fic.]
    Isbn 978-1-57433-047-2
    Printed in the United States of America

For Motto and Karbo, Gull and Bot,
and, always, Kate

In the forest of Burzee grows
The blood-red bloom of the Burzee Rose.
Its honey fire scents the air
Drawing creatures everywhere.
Blooms like fists, wounding thorns,
With saw-toothed emerald leaves adorned,
It numbs the nose and draws the skin
To touch and bleed and touch again.
  It is a wonder too behold,
  A present from the days of old.
  Still it grows in deep distress
  And every year it comes back less.

In a time already near
No one left will find it there.
Children in the woods for fun
Secret lovers on the run
Will miss the scent as they pass by.
Someday soon the rose will die.
  In the heart of Burzee grows
  The shrinking wonder of the rose.
  Find it, find it, while you may.
  The best things all will pass away.

1

CLAIRE DROPPED THE BAG OF FOOD on the table and took a burger for herself. "Food's here," she called out not quite loud enough for the whole house to hear but loud enough for anyone nearby. Word tended to spread pretty fast when a bag of food landed on the table.

When Morris descended on the kitchen—and he came directly, as he always did, being pretty hungry most of the time—Claire had already disappeared into the basement, where her office was, where she did most of her eating. Whatever else she did down there was a mystery, one Morris saw no particular need to explore. Claire was his third stepmother. They didn't tend to last.

Claire and his dad both said they hoped the children would learn to get along like brother and sister. But his dad had also said things that made Morris realize that this might be a waste of time. "That's just kind of the way things are today," he'd told him after his second stepmother left. "People don't stay together like they used to." But, really, that's something Morris already knew. There was hardly anyone at school who didn't have a step-someone in the house or who didn't move from house to house as the hormones attached and reattached from one partner to another. That didn't mean his house wasn't weird. It wasn't even that, as far as heritage went, they were a little United Nations (though not necessarily all that "united," but then neither was the United Nations if you thought about it). People are people. But then there was the one who wasn't related to anyone. That was Jasmine. She'd been picked up along the way by Claire, originally, she said, a stepdaughter of a guy who'd abandoned both of them so long ago Claire had actually changed the baby's name (though, looking at her, she couldn't be more than half Asian).

Tanya blew into the kitchen just as Morris was leaving. "She get any grilled chicken?" she called to Morris' retreating Nikes.

"How should I know?" Morris didn't turn around.

"Well you were just in the bag," she said as though Morris was still in the room.

"Just take what's on top," he yelled back.

"Like you don't even have a preference?"

Morris stuck his head back into the room. This was the longest conversation he'd had yet with his new stepsister. "It's *fast food*," he said, as though that explained something. But then, to the quizzical expression on her face he added, "there's only two flavors: mayonnaise or ketchup."

Tanya's response, if there was one, was overwhelmed by the tsunami of a blues progression that slammed in from down the hall, filling the kitchen and adjoining rooms: Jasmine, practicing.

"Would you tell your stepsister to tone it down?" Morris dug his fingers into his unbitten sandwich.

"She'd lose the sound."

"Then tell her use headphones. I've got stuff to do. I can't be…"

"And blow an eardrum? You want that? Then she'd have to turn it up even louder."

"Well she could at least tune the stupid guitar," he huffed.

Morris laid the *Call of Duty* box on the game console and pulled out the wires to hook up the new 64-inch plasma TV. This game was gonna be boss on this monster.

"You're not supposed to be playing that," said Tanya.

Why had she followed him into the room? Had she taken his quip about Jasmine's grating guitar as some kind of invitation?

"Like anyone's gonna notice."

"They said…"

"They say all sorts of crap. No follow through." And then, to Tanya's silence-thickening eyeball roll, "you didn't notice?"

"Claire's gonna have a cow."

"Claire's gonna be gone. You're all gonna be gone before Christmas."

And then the distortion from down the hall swelled and, poof, the screen went black, the air conditioner stopped, and the blues faded away.

"What the…" was all Morris managed to say before the sound of an explosion reverberated through the house. Morris and Tanya both jerked back like they'd been shot.

"I told you to tell your sister to turn that amp down."

"What?"

"Blew every circuit breaker in the house."

"As if."

And then Jasmine was in the room holding her guitar by the neck like it was a goose she'd just shot. "What the hell was that?"

Tanya went to the window, but in the middle of the day you couldn't really tell if the other houses had power. She listened. "He thinks you did it."

Jasmine laughed and swept the strings of her guitar. "Wouldn't that be cool?"

Morris ran out of the room with a purposeful motion that made Tanya and then Jasmine follow.

"No gas in the generator," he said when Tanya arrived in the garage.

"Then we gotta get some," Jasmine rounded the corner.

"You got a license?" said Tanya.

"Ask mom."

"She's working."

"How's she gonna work without power?" said Morris.

"Batteries. Cell phone," said Jasmine. "Personal hotspot."

Morris huffed. He knew that, of course. But when you're frustrated you've got to say something. "What does she do down there all day anyway?"

There was no response.

"I can't believe this." Morris exclaimed when the silence grew awkward. He grabbed the gas can. "I'm asking her."

"Good luck with that," said Jasmine.

"I had my whole day planned out," he said.

"You're not the only one," said Jasmine.

"Screw it, then. I'm walking."

"Like hell, you're walking. It's five miles to the nearest gas station," said Tanya. "By the time you get back, power'll be back on."

"Five gallons of gas, pretty heavy load to carry five miles." Jasmine shoved aside boxes still unpacked from the move. "Thought so," she said, revealing two bicycles, an old ten-speed and a mountain bike. The mountain bike had a rack and some frayed bungee cords. "Who's got money?"

They all looked at each other.

"I know where a credit card is," said Tanya.

"We can't use mom's credit card." Jasmine stared at Tanya.

"It's for gas. She buys gas all the time. She'll never notice."

Jasmine turned her head toward the closed garage door. "What if the power comes back on before we get back?"

"Yeah, but if it doesn't, you won't be able to play your guitar," said Morris.

"If the power comes on, I'll call you," said Tanya.

"Just give *me* the credit card," said Morris.

"As if," said Tanya.

"Maybe she won't notice," said Jasmine.

2

THE PURE TONE OF BOTTO'S BELL swelled like a bubble through the murmuring of elves. Everything went quiet. Motto hummed the note—E-flat above middle C. At the front of the crowded hall, Geimle paused mid-sentence and held his pose like a statue, his raised left hand clutching a rolled up piece of paper with which he seemed to be pointing to the second-floor mural of the Big Guy with sparkling eyes and an eight-foot grin. Geimle pivoted his head in the direction of Motto and Botto and peered over his glasses.

"Motto?" he said.

"Actually it was Botto," Motto pointed left with his thumb. "Mine's an F-sharp."

"Botto, then?" Geimle sounded like the frustrated shop teacher he'd been back when Botto's father was but a gleam in his grandmother's eye.

"Well, I was just thinking," Botto gestured, "what's the point? I mean, really, what's the point? It used to be kind of a joke, you know, 'Christmas in July,' because, you know, by July it had been *so long* since they'd thought about Christmas. But now, now July's just the new zero date on the Advent calendar, isn't it. Start of the new holiday season. By the time we're old like you, the holiday season won't even *be* a season. It'll just be—you know—the thing."

"The thing?"

"Starts back up in January. I'm just saying if we called it quits right now, today, and never delivered another present to another child anywhere in the world, would they even notice? Our part in this *holiday*, it's just an afterthought. It's like the part of the frosting that sticks to the fork after you've eaten the cake."

Geimle straightened his glasses and bunched his considerable lips and pushed them over to one side of his face as a dozen cogent replies sprang to mind. "The point, as I've said—you were listening, weren't you?—the point is to get it back. That's what the Big Guy wants. That's what he's asking for—if I read this note correctly, which I'm sure I do." Geimle unrolled the piece of paper in his hand. He stared at it and then turned the writing side toward Botto—though he was much too far away to read it. "Yes. You're right. As I've already explained, not only is our role in the holiday shrinking like an ice cap, but elves are leaving like rats from a sinking ship. That's why we're here. We have to fix what we can."

That bit about the rats might have been hyperbole, but elves *were* leaving. Although until now it had never been officially recognized, the number of workers in the factories was obviously diminishing—not rapidly, but steadily. Elves had been choosing to leave the noble work and (as the euphemism went) "return to Burzee." No one knew for sure how long this had been going on. But it had grown more obvious lately. As to why this was happening or where the missing elves were actually going, that was less clear. After finding, tacked to his office door, the anonymous note in his hand (probably in the Big Guy's handwriting), Geimle thought he understood: the great symphony of elven labor, replayed every year, culminating in the annual crescendo of Christmas, was not being heard any more; it was being drowned out in the great thundering cacophony that the holiday had become practically everywhere it was celebrated. The contribution of the elves went mostly unnoticed. So one by one, they were leaving in a downward spiral that made the work all that much harder to do—or to notice.

It was just a theory. But Geimle realized that if the Big Guy, sick as he was, was getting involved, something must be done.

And, no, he was not sure this was the proper something. How could he be?

He might have been more certain if he knew, at least, where the missing elves were actually going—if there was, indeed, one place they were actually going to. But you couldn't ask them because they didn't give notice. They just left. It was like someone was shushing them at the door. Maybe they *were* going in search of Burzee. Some elves still held out hope that the ancient elven homeland of Burzee had survived the human expansion. But not many. And where the old kingdom might be exactly, no one could recall. Some thought it was in Europe, some said South America, others located it at various other places all over the globe. Most elves would tell you it no longer existed anywhere, that "civilization" had razed it long ago. If an elf announced, "I'm going back to Burzee," it meant only, "I'm leaving. You won't see me again." They even left their phones behind. It was always sad. North Pole work had always been the best work an elf could do.

After ripping the admittedly puzzling note from the tack that had been rudely pushed into the ornate carving of his office door, Geimle decided the Big Guy was calling them to reclaim the holiday—and to entice his elves back home. Naturally, Geimle was all over that.

Standing in front of the all the elves of the West Wing, scratching his head with the rolled up note, Geimle tried to recall what else it was he'd meant to say. Then again, if he couldn't remember it, perhaps it wasn't that important. The plan had been laid out. And there was work to do.

He stood there like a plastic toy, slowly bobbling his head.

An F-sharp pierced his thoughts.

He frowned again. Perhaps it would have been better simply to give orders without wasting time on questions—the way old Dafle would have done it if he were still here.

"Whose idea was it to hand bells out anyway?" he muttered.

A polite laugh carried through the hall.

"Motto?"

"So I think what Botto's trying to say is maybe instead of, you know, expanding our reach, like you're saying with your otherwise certainly cutting-edge scheme, maybe we should be, you know, contracting."

"And why exactly do you think that's what Botto is saying?"

"Because it was *my* idea. He just kinda stole it."

"Please, everyone, we are at the end of our time. There is a lot of work to do. Put down your bells. The issue is not up for discussion. We've begun the process. I'm just keeping you informed."

The room went quiet; the quiet was broken by the perfect tone of Botto's E-flat.

"No more comments," said Geimle.

"Sir, I just don't think you've thought this through."

"No more comments," said Geimle.

But as soon as he turned his head, an F-sharp filled the room.

"What is it, Motto?"

"It was Botto. He grabbed my bell."

"I did not," said Botto. Motto grabbed Botto's bell and rang it like a fire alarm.

Botto grabbed Motto's and did the same.

The next morning, Motto and Botto found themselves assigned to the planer. Motto, of course, blamed Botto.

The two had spent many years in the mailroom, a pretty good job, more than half way through the ranks, and just a few steps below their dream jobs. Old friends, they did not talk about the incident of the bells for weeks. Then one morning, in the middle of the day, between shut down and re-start, Motto blurted out, "when I told you Geimle had a stupid idea, I wasn't asking you to *tell him* it was a stupid idea."

To which Botto coolly replied, "You didn't have to let on it was *your* idea, you know. I could be working the planer by myself."

"And let *you* run off with the credit? I don't think so."

"In that case, I have no idea what you're complaining about."

Botto rolled his eyes and stared out the window. Snow drifted around the reindeer barns. Motto stared at his friend through the long silence. Botto wiped his finger across the screen of his phone, pulled up an image of the same scene he was looking at out the window and zoomed in on the door. He could almost see, inside the barn, the pawing hoofs of the rows of reindeer in their stalls. Finally he looked up at Motto and let it out, "I thought it would get us promoted."

"Us?" said Motto.

"It's a brilliant observation. We'd be saving him months of labor, and all that delivery work. We have more work to do than ever before and now he's *adding* production? It makes no sense. I thought it would finally get us moved, you know, out of the mailroom."

"Yeah, well, mission accomplished."

"I meant *up.* "

"You thought shooting down Geimle's new plan that he's been working on for months right in front of the entire West Wing would get us promoted?"

"Who knew he had so much ego invested in his stupid idea?"

"Who *didn't* know?"

Motto switched on the machine.

They were both perfectly aware, of course, that planing wood remained a significant part of the complex toy making process in the Legacy Division of Claus Ltd. Screw that up, you get rough surfaces and splinters on your puzzles and trains. Still, it rankled. Geimle obviously meant the experience to be humbling. But it wasn't humbling. It was humiliating. Neither one understood why Claus, Ltd. even maintained, in this day and age, a Legacy Division. What kind of kid wants a circus wagon or a wooden train for Christmas? But more importantly, Botto and Motto had been convinced they'd left the planer permanently behind decades ago. Maybe they were still steps away from their dream jobs—Botto's was in Imagineering. He wanted to use his 8G eTab to imagine the shapes and functions of the toy lines of the future. For Motto the goal was musical instruments. He had an idea he was dying to try out for a software-enhanced, five-stringed fiddle for people with long thumbs—but the mailroom wasn't bad work.

"It's dead end," Botto said. "Elves that go to the mailroom don't always come out."

"Some of them like the mailroom," said Motto.

"Well, I don't. And neither do you."

"It sure beats the planer."

If Geimle was going to assign them to the menial task of planing—a task any octogenarian could do in his sleep—well, Botto decided, something would have to be done about it. Not only was the work strictly entry-level, it was boring as all get-out. And as for the noise—you could barely think when that monstrous contraption ground the last wrinkle and burr from the milled lumber. And you certainly couldn't talk. But that was by design. Hard to foment resistance when you can't spread the word.

"You can't say Geimle's not good at his job," Botto yelled over the high-pitched grinding. "Nonetheless, we're going to have to show him that more Christmas early in the year is just exactly the wrong way to go."

"I saw your mouth move but I have no idea what you said," Motto yelled back.

"Can I assume from the fact that you are obviously talking that you heard me and are shouting unconditional agreement?" yelled Botto.

"Well your hearing must be considerably better than mine. If I weren't looking directly at you, I wouldn't even know you were speaking," yelled Motto.

"Even if this machine were not using the full capacity of my ears with the sound like the grinding of cats, these foam plugs in my ears would render me deaf even to messages of a life-saving nature," yelled Botto. "Perhaps we should talk about this later."

"I'll have to turn the machine off if you want to talk to me. And you know what will happen if I do that." Motto couldn't even hear his own voice.

"Whatever you do, don't turn the machine off. They'll be on us in a second," yelled Botto.

The motor whined to a halt and Motto pulled the plugs out of his pointed ears.

"What is so…"

He could say no more before Philona was breathing beside them.

"Problem with the machine, boys?"

A suitable retort rose to Botto's lips but made it no further.

"Because I know of a couple openings in the reindeer stalls, compost division. Deadlines, boys, deadlines."

The machine whined back to life under Motto's forced smile as Philona mouthed something the two were just as happy not to hear.

3

THE BIG WINDOW of Giemle's office overlooked the factory floor. From there, he could see everything he needed to see: the planers, the shapers, the fabricators, the band saws, the bench saws, the router tables, the drill presses—all the trusty vintage machinery on which Claus Ltd. had established its worldwide reputation.

"It's like a snow globe," he said. "We could model that and sell it."

"If sawdust were snow," Karble smiled without looking up from her work.

"I don't need monitors," he said. "Why would anyone think I need monitors? Why would the Big Guy think I need monitors?"

Karble's recip saw whirred to life. Geimle tried to raise his voice over the clatter.

"I've got this great big window up here, and I've got Philona down there."

"I just do what I'm told, sir," she said.

"Why do we suddenly need all these electronics everywhere?"

"Just keeping up with the times, I imagine, sir."

"With a bank of bubble monitors?"

"We had them left over, sir." Karble measured the space.

"This technology must be thirty years old. One flat screen on a rotating scan—that would be more than enough. Does the Big Guy think things will run smoother if I don't have to get up from my desk?"

"That certainly may be it, sir."

"I have to get out up from my desk to see the monitor. I *like* getting up from my desk."

Karble turned toward him for the first time and flashed a look that quickly ran from sympathy to resignation before it fell into indifference.

A whistled chorus of an old Burzee folk song wafted in from the hall as into the office strolled Malveno, Geimle's boyhood friend, now head of the East Wing, Polymer Fabrication.

"Ha," he said. "Just look at us—managers!"

"This just hitting you now? I haven't made a hobby horse since we almost lost old Dasher to the croup—and that would have to have been the current Dasher's grandsire at least."

"Yeah, well I was reminded of the change when I passed the planer."

"You heard about that little dust up?" Geimle tapped on the long window. A crooked expression settled on Malveno's face.

"Heard about it? Watched it happen."

Geimle was confused.

Malveno looked over at Karble, "Sure did. Didn't I, Karble?"

"Monitors in his office too, sir."

"Been waiting for you to bring it up, in fact."

"You think I should ask for your opinion on every little decision?"

"You mean like you always have?"

Geimle leaned his back against the glass of the big window and said nothing.

"When I saw those guys flailing away on those bells, I thought, hey, wasn't that us—just a little while ago? Remember—the troublemakers we used to be?"

"You think sixty years is a little while?"

"It's all relative," Malveno said.

"Why are they broadcasting *my* meeting on a monitor in *your* office?"

Malveno shrugged.

"Anyway, *we* didn't ring bells," said Geimle.

"I warned you about those bells." Malveno chuckled. "How many times did we get stuck on the planer because we couldn't shut our mouths?"

A half smile rose on Geimle's face, but it was quickly overtaken by a half-pained, half-tired expression.

"You know why you're doing this to them, don't you?" Malveno said.

"Because they were undermining morale?"

"Because you know they're right. We're less relevant every year."

"Yes," Geimle threw up his hands. "That's the problem. That was the whole point of the meeting. It's not Motto and Botto's point. It's what *I've* been saying. It's what I've been saying for a long time."

"Hey, hey, calm down. Point is, like they said, this plan of yours, well, it's a little cock-eyed."

"Well you don't recover your relevance by doing *less,* do you? Pull back? Close shop? Just let the shrinking ice cap suck us down? Is that a good idea?"

"But what can we really do about it? People—human people—they've taken practically the whole operation away from us already. I say this problem is a whole lot bigger than Claus, Ltd."

"And I say we *can* do something about it. What possible good could it do to say we can't? This comes down from the Big Guy himself, you know."

"So I've heard. And now you want to plant Christmas all over the world in the off season?"

"To recover it, the thing itself, the *real* purpose of our being here."

"You can see how that might feed into the very problem you're trying to solve."

"It's not just Christmas—it's old-style Christmas. The essence. It's how it was when it was good."

"The *ideal* Christmas? The fantasy Christmas? Christmas like it never was!"

"I don't know if I'd use those terms."

"The thinner the ice, the faster the melting," Malveno chuckled.

Geimle huffed. "*Little* reminders." He hunted for a new way to say this. "Tickling the subconscious." He rolled his eyes. "Anyway, until I get a better idea, this is it. I just need the troops on my side."

Malveno walked over to the window and gazed down at the workspace. "They're elves. They'll pretty much do whatever you tell them to do."

"Providing they don't go tromping off to Burzee. Providing the Mottos and the Bottos and—and the Malvenos out there don't rile them up."

"You're going to be forcing overtime. Last I saw, you had just one bag of prototypes. Plus, you're going to have to enter the vortex off season. More time, more expenses. What's exactly did the Big Guy say when you talked about this?"

"Still sick, I'm afraid."

"You mean you haven't actually discussed it with him? You pulled this whole plan out of that enigmatic, unsigned note?" He pointed to the curled piece of paper tacked to a bulletin board.

"Not to be disturbed. Have you tried to get into the castle?"

"Though he's not too sick to order cameras and monitors in every corner of the estate." Malveno nodded over to Karble, who smiled without looking back as she hoisted a screen. He went over to the corkboard and stared at the note, "and not too sick to tack a mysterious note to your door."

He pulled it from the tack:

> *Who spends a fortune for a pennyworth of fun?*
> *Who constructs sand castles in a thunder storm?*
> *What good is a toy too complex to play with?*
> *Why water the Burzee Rose after it has dropped its seed?*

"It's not even a note. It's just questions. Are you even sure this is the Big Guy's handwriting?"

"It was tacked to the door."

"Yes, but by whom?"

Karble's drill whined loudly behind them.

"Some elf on his way to Burzee I imagine—offering this instead of an explanation. Someone picked it up at the castle—and, yes, it's clearly the Big Guy's handwriting—and brought it down and tacked on my door on the way out. The meaning's pretty clear," said Geimle.

"You think? Wonder what cloudy would look like." Malveno scratched his head. "So your theory is that someone went to the castle to see the Big Guy and got turned away. Then this mystery elf found this 'note' just lying around somewhere and he or she realized that the Big Guy himself was having doubts about the future of the whole enterprise and so she or he tacked the note on your door so that you'd understand what was really going on and why all these elves were fading into the sunset, all in the hope you'd do something to stop it?"

"Basically."

"Why would anyone do that?"

"You got a better explanation?"

"I imagine I could come up with *another* explanation. I mean, if we're just making stuff up. You sure we can't just ask the Big Guy?"

"No doing. Place is guarded like a fortress. Last Christmas took a lot out of him."

"So we're just going behind his back," Malveno scratched his head, "—on mere speculation?"

"I wouldn't put it that way."

"Dangerous weather there, hiding something this big from *himself.*"

"It's not like we don't have the authority."

"It's a little bit like we don't have the authority."

A crash and a quick shriek from the corner.

"So sorry. I don't know what happened. I've never..." At Karble's feet lay scattered pieces of a broken monitor. "It slipped."

"Marble floor," Malveno chuckled. "Hard as ice and just as cold. Not the Big Guy's best notion."

"Didn't want it anyway," said Geimle. "Just clean it up."

Karble clipped the wires.

"You've always got Philona," said Malveno.

"Always got Philona for what?" said Philona, just that moment coming through the arched doorway.

"For keeping the floor on schedule," said Geimle. "Malveno tells me Motto and Botto are really taking to their new job."

"Taking to? As in enjoying?" She wrinkled her mouth. "I couldn't say. But they are certainly *doing* their new job. Might take the mistletoe out of 'em in another month or two."

Before the snicker dissipated, Karble had made it to the door.

"Where are you going?"

"You don't want me here working during your meeting, sir."

"There won't be any secrets at a production meeting. Do clean up the mess."

"Of course," she said, "I just need some… stuff." She raised a finger and scurried out the door.

Geimle looked at Malveno.

"Well, *I'm* not cleaning it up."

"Seemed in an awful hurry," said Philona as more supervisors and managers began to arrive.

"Shy," said Geimle. "Just shy."

4

BOTTO PEERED INTO THE REINDEER STALLS. If Karble had managed to knock out that monitor while everyone was gathering around Geimle's waxed oak table, they had perhaps a half hour before they'd be missed.

"Why are we doing this?" Motto whispered.

"I told you. We're going to show everyone Geimle's plan won't work."

"Yeah, but how? You didn't tell me how you were going to show them."

"Shhhh."

Haymin, the stable manager, would also be at the meeting in Geimle's office by now. And none of the stable elves were in sight. Still, Motto followed Botto on tiptoe to Dasher's stall.

"You also didn't tell me why I'm following you."

"Shhhh," Botto repeated as he rose to his tiptoes and peered up and down. "Because I can't do it alone. You get Vixen."

"Do what alone?"

Botto petted Dasher's muzzle as he carefully unhooked the rope that was holding him in the stall.

"Show Geimle his plan won't work. Are you paying attention?"

"You have no idea what you're doing, do you? You have no plan of any kind!"

"Some of the details are still a bit fuzzy."

"Hey!"

Motto and Botto turned at the sound of a voice.

"Karble?" Motto called out. Motto was sweet on Karble.

"Hey, Motto."

"Shhhhh. You guys understand, we're not supposed to be here, right? We clear, Karble?"

"Yeah, for a minute, grumpy face, until they notice I haven't got back to clean up the mess. *YES,* I had to break the monitor or they would've wondered why I took so long to hook it up. Do you really expect this cockamamie plan to work? How are we gonna stay out of trouble? They're not stupid. One of them is going to look out the window."

"What?" Motto tried to break into the speech. "You're in on this sleigh-wreck of a scheme?"

"Ten minutes is all we need," said Botto. "We've certainly got ten minutes."

"Unless he looks out the window," said Karble.

"Why would he look through the window when he has three working monitors?" Geimle led Dasher through the door onto the snow. It was pretty clear no one was around to see them just now.

"Which show every station *except* the planer?" Motto asked.

Botto smiled at his brilliance. "Have you got the sacks?"

Karble made a come-here motion toward end of the barn. "You didn't exactly give me a lot of time."

Gullnle appeared from behind the barn dragging two large velvet sacks, one maroon, the other forest green.

"Gully?" said Botto. "What are you doing here?"

"You didn't expect me to get the bags while I was pretending to install a monitor, now, did you?" said Karble, "master plan-man."

"You seem a little nervous, Karble," said Botto.

"What do you mean pretending?" said Motto.

"Well, to make it look real, I had to actually install them."

23

"I thought you were supposed to install all these monitors anyway," said Botto.

"Of course I am. That's not the point."

"Wait, wait, I'm confused," said Motto.

"We're all confused," said Botto.

"No, no. I understand completely," said Gullnle

"Well then explain it me," said Motto.

"Stop it," said Karble. "We're wasting time. My job just isn't that interesting to people who aren't doing it. The point is, Geimle looked so suspicious it made me…"

"There's nothing suspicious," said Botto. They would've put monitors in there anyway, sooner or later. They're everywhere."

"You think I don't know that? Who do you think's putting these monitors in everywhere?"

Motto patted Karble on the back to calm her down.

Botto lifted himself onto Dasher. "Running late here. Climb up, Motto."

Motto climbed onto Vixen. Karble and Gully handed a sack to each of them and helped secure it behind the riding blanket in a harness made for the purpose.

"Where am I supposed to sit?" asked Gully.

"You're not going," said Botto.

"I'm not? Why not? You mean to tell me I snuck away over here, risked my job and practically threw my back out for those sacks, and I'm not even invited?"

"I think that's what he's saying," said Motto.

"Well, I don't think so."

"I have to clean up the mess," Karble mumbled. She insisted Motto and Botto climb back down off the reindeer so she could give them a good-bye hug. Meanwhile Gullnle ran into the stables to get herself a reindeer.

"You have to stay here," Botto called to her. "We don't need three. There's only two sacks."

"I'll be right back." She disappeared behind the door.

"Should we wait for her?" asked Motto.

"No time," said Botto, and he pointed to the opposite end of the barn where two figures with manure rakes were standing, frozen, staring at them.

"Should we tell her?" said Motto.

"Oh, I think she'll find out pretty quick," said Botto. He patted Dasher on the rump as the two barn elves started running toward them. Dasher leaped into the sky with Vixen at his heels.

5

MOTTO PULLED VIXEN UP ALONGSIDE DASHER. "Did you bring the harp?"

"It's in the green bag."

"And the blue flame?"

"It's with the harp," said Botto. "Karble got them."

"What if Karble told Gully to get them?" said Motto.

"Then Gully got them." But Botto didn't sound absolutely sure about this.

"And the key?"

"Better check." Botto frowned.

"Oh, sure. As we pass the 3479 mile marker, we decide it's high time we find out if we packed."

"Are you muttering?"

Motto turned around and pulled the tie on the bulging green sack while Botto kept his eye out for the landing site.

"Should be all together in the same place," said Botto. But Motto wasn't finding them.

"Right on top," Botto added a note of strained optimism to his voice.

"If they were 'right on top' I think I would have seen them by now."

The bag was large and seemed to be even larger once you reached your hands in, as though it held way more than its actual capacity. But it wasn't infinite. Motto mumbled again and pulled out a blue object shaped like a brick and was almost as heavy. It was beeping.

"What the heck is this?"

He tossed it to Botto. Botto chuckled as it fell into his lap. Botto wasn't very good at catching things. "You are *so* lucky." Botto picked up the cold, metallic brick. He had no idea what it was until he read the word "tracker" embossed on the end in small letters above a glass circle beside another small circle that was red—and flashing.

"Oh, the blest North Winds," said Botto, "They're tracking us."

"Who?"

"And this, this must be a lens." Botto turned the device over again. He put what he thought was a lens up to his eye as though perhaps if he put the effort in he could see back through to whoever might be watching. "And I'll bet this grill is a microphone."

"Who? Who's tracking us? Geimle? Karble? The Big Guy?"

"No idea."

"You know this scheme of yours just keeps getting better. I can just see the welcoming committee now. Probably right there on the ground by the vortex with the flame and the harp and the key. A whole throng of...."

"Yeah, but once we're *in* the vortex...."

"We don't have the key!" Motto huffed. "What's lower than shoveling reindeer crap?"

But Botto's attention had already turned back to the tracker. "Maybe we can find some way to turn it off... I mean, if it's not too late."

Botto tossed it back to Motto, who was much better with electronics and with catching things. Motto flipped it over a few times. "There's no switch. Got any other ideas?"

Botto thought a minute. "Yes. Yes, I have. Toss it back."

Motto raised his eyebrows and smirked but did as requested. "Two for two?" Botto, however, made no motion to catch the thing. It bounced off Dasher's flank and wafted through the air like a heavy leaf in the direction, he guessed, of Indiana.

"Oops!" Botto chuckled.

"What if there was someone down there?" said Motto.

"What are the chances?"

It wobbled through the clouds and then it fell out of sight. In another few seconds a little ball of light could be seen which was followed about ten second later by a popping sound.

"Well that was unexpected," said Botto. "Suppose it was a bomb?"

"We don't make bombs," said Motto. "Probably hit something."

"Like what? A munitions dump?"

And then Motto went back to the bag to search for the missing items.

"Karble is very reliable," said Botto, as though that proved the things were in the sack.

"Yes, and Gully is well meaning. However," Motto was going to let the rest of the thought take care of itself, but then concluded, "they're just not in here." Motto looked up with heavy eyes and sighed.

Motto took his hands out of the sack and stared into it.

"And I went through all the trouble to make those marzipan replicas. Doesn't that always happen? You concoct a perfect plan. You work out every detail and then something breaks down anyway?"

"Yes," said Motto. "It *always* happens. Not that I have any reason to think your plan wasn't perfect, but you'd think you'd learn."

"We're so close. We're practically at the door." Botto pulled out his phone.

"What are you doing?"

"What if I just call Karble and have her bring the stuff? Rendezvous in Manitoba or something."

"Sure, throw away the tracking device and *then* turn on your phone on the off chance that every elf north of the Canadian wilderness doesn't already know where we are. Let's just invite them all down like a blizzard."

"I don't think you can invite a blizzard."

They landed in a little wooded area somewhere near the invisible door to the time vortex. They'd both given the green sack another thorough going over without finding the items they'd need to precisely locate and enter the door.

Botto conked himself on the head with the flat of his hand. Motto went over to Dasher and opened the maroon sack. And there, right on top, was the package with the harp and the flame and the key.

"She put them the wrong sack," Botto's eyes grew wide.

"Did you tell her which sack to put them in?"

"One for supplies; one for toys. It should have been obvious."

6

"HEARD?" GEIMLE SAID. "Heard? From whom? Who told you they were going somewhere?"

"How many elves know about this?" Malveno half smiled at the image of a platoon of young elves infiltrating the globe with gifts.

"Let me rephrase that," said Gullnle. "I didn't really 'hear' about them going. I *saw* them going to the barns. Yes, 'heard they were planning' was definitely a figure of speech. I saw them go to the barns and I followed them because I knew they were supposed to be at the planer at that time of day and I tried to chase after them— to bring them back like responsible elves concerned about their futures. But those do-rights in the barns…"

"Hang on, hang on." Philona went to Geimle's desk and pulled up the work manifest. "Where were you that you saw them go to the barns? You work in the, ah, yes, in Factory North, do you not? 'Package design' it says here. How could you *see* them going to the barns?"

"Something's going on," said Geimle. "Something very odd is going on here."

"Let's not jump to conclusions," said Malveno. "Couple of pranksters off on a lark could explain the whole thing."

"Elves don't act like this," said Philona.

"*We* would have, if we'd thought of it. You know very well we would have."

"You're not helping," said Geimle.

"So how could you possibly have seen them go to the barns if you were at work?" Philona repeated.

Gullnle scratched her neck, then rubbed her cheeks and squinted. "Well," she said, "you don't *really* think something's going on, do you? Why would something be going on? What does that even mean?" And she looked across the room to where Karble was replacing the monitor she'd broken that morning. Karble, staring at her, raised her eyebrows and tilted her head at the bank of screens. "And as for your intelligent query," Gullnle said to Philona. "Umm. We have a monitor focused on the reindeer barns up in package design. Yeah, that's it."

"Who is ordering all these blasted monitors all of a sudden?" Geimle said.

"What possible reason could anyone have to order a monitor of the reindeer barns in package design?" Philona asked.

"It's gotta be the Big Guy," said Malveno, "he does things like that. He's very unpredictable."

"Well, there's unpredictable, and then there's just flat out crazy," said Geimle.

"I agree." Gullnle was starting to believe she was going to get through this interrogation without being reassigned to menial work—and maybe even without having to rat out Karble. "It must have been the Big Guy. I mean, I don't really need to see the…. but I did see them, sure as the Big Guy's snowy beard I…."

"Karble," Philona interrupted, "who gave you your orders? You report directly to the Big Guy, do you?"

"What? Well, I…"

"That's impossible," said Geimle. "She's not a manager. If she reported directly…"

"Well, what I was going to say was…."

"Yes?"

"…I assume the orders I received came from… well, they came from…" and she raised her hand as high over her head as she could reach. "At least I think they did. I think definitely they could have done that. But not to me of course, not directly, I mean. I of course got them from… from the ordinary chain of command."

"The real question," Gullnle cut in, "is what are we going to do about Motto and Botto? I think we've got to focus here."

"They're already assigned to the planer," said Philona.

"I say we send someone after them," said Gullnle. "I'll go."

"You'll go?" said Geimle. "Where will you go?"

"Earth's a pretty big place to lose an elf," said Malveno.

"Do you know something you're not telling us?"

Gullnle managed to talk for another hour without revealing any information. She winked at Karble as she headed for the door.

Geimle turned to Malveno and Philona when she was gone. "What are they up to? Why would two young elves run south in the off season, in the middle of the day, with reindeer? They know the risks."

"Looking for Burzee?" Philona asked.

But Geimle and Malveno ruled that out. "They're young and ambitious," said Geimle. "They're not like the bunch we see running for the homeland. They don't know what's really going on."

"Do you?" Philona stared at her supervisor.

"No," he said. "I don't."

Philona looked over at Karble who seemed to be focused intently on her wiring. "Karble." She had to repeat her name with increasing volume: "Karble!"

Karble jumped. "Sorry."

"What's taking you so long to wire one monitor?"

"No idea. Begging your pardon, ma'am. The darn thing won't turn on. I think it may be a dud."

Philona walked over to the young elf and stared down at the equipment. "Try pushing the on button," she said.

A feed of the idle planer filled the screen. Karble smiled shyly, mumbled, bowed, grabbed her tools, and scurried out the door.

"You don't suspect Karble?" asked Geimle.

"At this point, I suspect everyone," said Philona.

"Why didn't we ever hijack reindeer?" said Malveno.

"And gone where?" said Geimle.

"I have no idea. But grabbing reindeer and heading to the springtime. Why weren't we that bold when we were young enough to do it?"

"Perhaps you observed the line between prankish and reckless," said Philona.

Geimle stood in front of the new array of technologically out of date monitors as though the answer lay somewhere in these ordinary images. Philona walked over to see what he was looking at.

There was nothing on the monitors that deserved their attention. Certainly she should know. They were all focused on her floor.

"I'm sure you've tried their phones," said Malveno.

"Off, of course, or left behind. They can't be traced," said Geimle.

"How do we find them?"

"We don't," said Geimle. "We have no idea where they are. We can't spare enough elves to scour the earth. And can you imagine if we did? One or two elf sightings and the humans laugh it off. Hundreds running around in broad daylight and something's going to happen."

"Yes, but…" Philona began.

"Wouldn't you love to have something happen?" said Malveno.

"Besides," Geimle went on, "with the Big Guy incapacitated along with everything else, there's that much more to do." Geimle's voice was edged more with pleading than conviction.

"If I may, Geimle, we also have no idea what they are up to. Something may happen if we don't look for them."

"That is a risk. But I don't think it's very big one. You heard Gullnle. If she was part of the scheme and she had no real idea what they were up to, I assume the scope is pretty limited. What can two elves do in that great big world?"

"Unless she knows more than she managed to say."

"I admit, there was a good deal more talking than saying," said Malveno. "But still…"

"Unless something else happens to change our plan, I say we let them go. They'll have to come back eventually. We can deal with them then."

Malveno kept staring at the screens. Karble briefly crossed into view near the planer then passed out of sight through a doorway. "Question," he said, "where does that doorway lead?" He pointed to the monitor where he'd seen Karble pass.

"Outside," said Philona. "South, toward the barns."

"But isn't maintenance in the North Wing?" said Malveno. "Why is Karble heading that way?" He pressed a button on one of the other monitors several times until the reindeer barn appeared.

There in the middle of the screen, just passing through the barn door was Gullnle, leading Prancer into the yard.

Geimle grabbed his phone and quick-dialed Haymin.

Just then Karble entered the picture. Running full tilt toward Gullnle, she grabbed the reins and held on. Both become quickly animated. And then Haymin stood in the barn door with his phone to his ear. He whistled so loud Geimle had to lower his phone. Karble, startled, dropped the reins. Gullnle, freed, kicked Prancer to get her going. But the obedient reindeer just turned around and walked Gullnle back to Haymin. Through the phone they heard Haymin sooth the deer and scold the elf.

"Please invite Gullnle and Karble back to my office." Geimle hung up the phone. On the monitor, they watched Haymin snicker.

7

MORRIS STRUGGLED UP THE HILL. Sweat poured into his eyes, a twinge shot through each thigh every time he pressed his weight onto the pedals. He could feel his heart and his lungs in ways he could not remember ever feeling them before. Meanwhile Jasmine with her light frame of dry sticks flew up the hill like she was motorized. Sirens called from the distance.

"C'mon, c'mon... Oh," she said, pulling suddenly on the handbrakes. Her bike stopped but remained balanced several seconds before she put a foot to the pavement—a trick Morris wouldn't even try. The sirens grew closer.

"What is it?" he called.

"Well I guess I see why the power's out," said Jasmine. Just then two fire engines roared past them followed by two police cars.

"Fire," she said. And then he could smell the smoke. "That would be where the power comes from, I guess—a transformer or a substation or whatever they call it. Must've exploded or something."

Morris pulled up beside Jasmine, put his feet on the pavement and breathed deeply, glad for the break.

"Well if that's the case, we're *really* gonna need the generator." Fixing something like that—who knew how long that could take? As they neared the area, a cop with white gloves pointed them south. "Detour," she said and nodded to indicate she had nothing further to say. There was no point in protesting.

"Well that just about triples the distance to the gas station," said Morris. This meant that by the time he got the generator running again, his father might well be home and it would be a whole nother day before he'd have a chance to put *Call of Duty* on the big screen. It also meant his father could go out and get the gas for the generator himself. But would he? His father was the kind of guy who might decide to call it an adventure.

"You thinking of giving up?" Jasmine asked.

"By the time we get back with the gas, my dad'll be home with the car..."

"Yeah but what are you gonna do between now and then if you go back—read a book?"

An expression of horror flashed involuntarily across Morris' face.

"Hey, if you don't have what it takes to go 15 miles..."

"Don't be stupid," he said.

He wished he'd thought to bring a water bottle.

From the comfort of a car, the Indiana ground seems utterly flat. But on a bicycle every small gradation announces itself with an extra pain in the legs. He stopped near the woods by a ball field where a game was in progress. Jasmine was a half mile ahead before she turned around to check on him, yelled something, and then pedaled back.

"Break," he said, getting off the bike.

"If you can't do this," Jasmine began.

"Just thirsty," he said, pulling his leg over the crossbar. "And I got sweat pouring in my eyes."

"You know the purpose of eyebrows is to prevent that."

"Yeah, well it isn't working." Morris dug his palms into his eye sockets. His legs felt a little like the bolts needed tightening. For a split second he felt as though he would slosh onto the ground. Jasmine's tone changed suddenly. "Hey," she said, "just have a seat. Break is a good idea." And she slipped herself off her bike. "I'll go ask those people if they've got any water."

"I'll go with you," Morris said, shifting his weight as though to stand back up.

"You guard the bikes."

As far as Morris was concerned anyone who wanted to steal the bikes could have them. Still, he accepted the excuse. Jasmine took off across the field on her very thin legs. How she could store so much energy in so slight a frame, Morris had no idea.

Morris blinked to clear his eyes. Over to the right in the woods something moved. He couldn't quite tell what, but it wasn't... no, actually it was... It was a deer. It was *two* deer, big blocky deer, moving from tree to tree. But there was something else there too, smaller than the deer, hard to make out. But it was rushing around. As Jasmine went from person to person in the ball field (something that Morris found almost as interesting as whatever it was that was happening in the woods because he could hardly imagine himself thirsty enough to go around begging water from strangers), the deer paced back and forth sniffing the trees as though they were looking for something. Maybe they were smelling the bark to see what else had been this way lately. What did Morris know about the habits of deer? But it did seem odd. And then it appeared that the other things with the deer were people—children by the size of them. Well, he did know enough about deer to know *that* was odd.

Jasmine raced back, drinking from one water bottle and carrying another. "Scored two," she said.

"I can't believe you did that."

"I offered to pay for 'em. Nice people, though. Once they finished their double take. They just gave 'em to me." Jasmine's eyebrows shot up in self-satisfied way.

"I just wouldn't... What double take?"

"The one you people always do when someone who looks like Madame Chang speaks like Jenny Smith," she said. "You're welcome, by the way."

"Huh? Oh, sure. Thanks." Morris screwed up his face and raised his bottle and lowered it without drinking. "What do you mean 'you people'?"

"You playing with me?" she asked.

"Who's Madame Chang?"

"Never mind."

"I mean I probably would've been okay."

"You were like dying. Your face is red as a... just drink your water."

"I didn't do a double take."

"Of course you did."

Morris held the bottle to his lips. He looked past the clear plastic cylinder at Jasmine, squinting back at him. He lowered the bottle. "I did not."

"Looked at me like I was an alien from Mars."

"I do that to everyone."

"Yeah, well, everyone does it to me, rittle Chinee girr speak perfick Ingrish. I don't know enough Chinese to read a stop sign. I don't even know my own freaking name for God's sake."

Morris took a big drink. "Well *I* never thought twice about it," he said. "I mean, lots of people adopt foreign babies, Indian kids, black kids, Russian kids."

"Whatever," she said.

"Well, if you want to talk about it."

"I really don't."

"Then why'd you bring it up?"

Morris took another drink after which he pointed with a nod to the woods behind her. "See that?"

Jasmine stared. "Hey, let's check it out."

"I gotta guard the bikes."

"Take the stupid bike with you." And she frowned—she had a very expressive face—and grabbed her bike and got on it and lightly pedaled across the uneven and slightly damp ground. Morris would sink in like a stone if he tried that. He just knew it. But weightless Jasmine pushed off with ease, like she was pushing off the dock in a canoe. Morris breathed deep and pulled himself up. He walked his bike. His legs still didn't feel quite normal.

8

GULLY ANSWERED EVERY SINGLE QUESTION, told them everything they wanted to know.

Karble had managed to convince them that she herself was ignorant of the Motto and Botto's plan. They'd separated the two of them. First they talked to Karble and then asked her to sit in the inner office while they talked to Gullnle. They thought they'd sent Karble away. But she went back to the large storage closet in the old cartography suite where she worked. She liked to call this closet her office. From there she activated the new monitors in Geimle's office and heard the whole thing. Karble had told them that she'd seen an image of Motto and Botto running to the reindeer barns and, like a good elf, had gone after them to keep them out of trouble. But Gully spilled like a stool pigeon.

"How could you have told them everything?" said Karble. "You don't even know everything."

"They were gonna put me on wrapping paper."

"They *should* put you on wrapping paper."

"I don't mean wrapping-paper design, Karble. I mean actual wrapping paper. As in covering boxes and applying tape."

"I know what you meant. And I know what I said. I'm surprised you didn't tell them I was in on it."

"They didn't ask about that."

Karble wrinkled her lips and looked particularly displeased.

"Really," said Gully. "They didn't."

"But you would've told if they'd asked."

"So what are we going to do now?"

"What can we do? We can't warn them. We can't go after them. They're on their own."

"Well," said Gully, "we could always tell the Big Guy that Geimle and Malveno have stolen reindeer and gone rogue."

"We can't do that."

"Well, why not?"

"First of all," said Karble, "because he's sick in bed. Second of all because it wouldn't help. And third of all because it isn't true."

"Well they talked about it. Same thing."

"They're managers. They're *authorized* to take the reindeer—which they didn't even do. Why'd you put a tracker in the sack anyway?" Karble asked.

"In case they didn't want to take me with them—which they didn't."

"Where'd you even get a tracker?"

"It was in your locker."

"You stole my tracker!" Karble gasped. "I was still working on that. It's a prototype."

"It passed its first field test. Until it stopped. My only thing is, I don't know what happened. It doesn't have a visible off switch and it had fresh batteries. It worked all the way to the center of America and then, bammo, it just stopped. Did I miss a setting? Very strange."

"Yeah, I heard. Very convenient. It stopped practically on the door of the vortex. Now, Geimle and Malveno know exactly where they were headed, thanks to you."

"Well why *don't* they go get them?"

"They don't think Motto and Botto have the key. They said that after you left. They don't think they can enter the vortex. Philona checked the case."

"The key's still in it?"

"Not really, not the real… Hey, why am I telling you? You told them everything."

"How was I supposed to know that would happen?"

"You didn't have to tell them you'd planted a tracker." Karble shook her finger at Gully.

"They were going to put me on wrapping paper!"

9

"THEY'RE FRIENDLY." Jasmine petted the neck of one of the deer as Morris pulled up. It stood there fearlessly like a well-trained dog or a horse. "They're tame."

"Where are the people?" Morris went over and touched the deer's neck. The hair that looked smooth and soft was really course and bristly. It gave off a strong, wild smell like a very dusty room in a very old house.

"No idea," she said. "But they left some stuff, look."

She pointed to a large green bag on a big red blanket that was laid out as though for a picnic. Beside the bag were two harnesses, ornate leather with ball-shaped golden bells.

"So they're reindeer," said Morris. "Explains why they look funny."

"Why would anyone bring reindeer into the woods?"

"The obvious question," said Morris. "How'd they even get here? Reindeer are not exactly native to Indiana."

"And then abandon them here and dress them up like it was Christmas."

"Probably ran off when they saw you coming."

"You saying it's the people that aren't tame? Probably criminals."

"Part of that big reindeer ring. I'll bet we could ride 'em," Morris judged his chances of jumping onto the deer's back.

"The owners are obviously coming back. Must be part of a show or… hey, maybe they're making a movie."

"Then we better hurry up. Put the harness on. Way better than using those old bikes. Let the animals do the work."

"You ever ridden a reindeer?"

"I've never even ridden a horse. But I assume it's about the same."

"How's that supposed to matter if you've never done it?"

"You have a very expressive face," he said.

"What's *that* supposed to mean?"

"I'm just saying. I think eyebrows are for talking with. I don't buy the whole 'sweat blocker' thing."

"Whatever," she shook her head.

Morris looked the animal over as though there might be a step somewhere on its belly to help him climb aboard. The deer just stood there, breathing. "How do you suppose it works," he finally said.

"If you think I'm gonna help you steal someone else's reindeer…"

"You can't own a reindeer. It's a wild animal."

"You can own a harness, can't you?"

"We'll leave them the bikes for collateral. Help me get on."

"I just said…" Jasmine held a hand in the air and put the features of her face on pause along with her sentence.

Morris laughed. "I'm not gonna steal it. I just want to sit on it, maybe make it walk or something. You can't say that wouldn't be fun. You don't have to be quite so serious. What could happen? The owner comes and yells at us or something. Big deal. Act sad. Now help me on."

Jasmine huffed and rolled her eyes, but she approached Morris and the deer and she interlaced her fingers for Morris to use as a step. "Can't believe I'm doing this."

The reindeer didn't move. It just stood there through several very awkward attempts to throw a leg over its back as though it did this sort of thing all the time. With much struggle Morris finally laid his stomach across the deer's spine and with what appeared to be more a swimming than a climbing motion managed to squirm himself into place and sit like a cowboy on the back of the oblivious steed.

When Jasmine brought the bridle, the deer bowed its head.

"I don't think it's a wild animal," said Jasmine.

"Here goes." Morris grabbed the bridle and kicked his heels into the side of the deer.

It raised its head and seemed to stretch its neck.

"Did it just yawn?" said Jasmine.

Morris tried again. The reindeer grunted.

"Maybe I'm supposed to hit it or something. It's not a horse, you know."

"Maybe you better get down." Jasmine backed up.

Morris slapped the deer's flank. It was like slapping a bale of hay. Nothing happened. He slapped again, harder. He slapped as hard as he could. His hand hurt. The deer didn't move.

"Maybe it's animatronic," he said.

"Does it smell animatronic?"

True, the feral odor probably would be hard to imitate even if you wanted to.

"Maybe you better get down for real."

"I don't know what you're nervous about. It's not doing anything." And then he grabbed the antlers like handle bars. The deer shook its head. Hard. Before he could let go, Morris was pulled forward and tossed to the ground within inches of the animal's front hooves. He landed on his side and rolled onto his back. The deer put a paw to his chest and leaned its head down and stuck its nose in Morris's face.

Jasmine let out a yelp. She felt an impulse to cover her face with her hands. But she ran over to the deer to try to push it off Morris. She ran into it full force. It absorbed her like a rubber wall and threw her onto the ground.

Morris tried to roll out from under the hoof, but it held him there. If it put its foot down, it could have crushed his chest. But it seemed to know what it was doing. It just held him there as the second deer wandered over and lowered its muzzle. From where Jasmine sat it looked as though they were thirsty and Morris was the trough, or worse, as though they were hungry.

The second deer sneezed.

"Yuck! Deer snot! Help me get this foot off."

And then a voice that was high but oddly grumbly came from behind them. "Vixen!"

And the deer raised its foot and Morris rolled out and grabbed his side, which he now realized was in significant pain. He and Jasmine turned toward the voice.

"We weren't gonna hurt it," she said before she'd had time to take in who or what she was talking to.

"Looks more like she was gonna hurt you," said a very boy-sized man with a large head. He was dressed in green leather with elaborate embroidering, a costume that he must have thought fit with the reindeer for whatever show or exhibition or movie they were about. And he had dark skin. Not African, or Indian or Native American even; it had a tinge she had never seen before, but it was hard to tell since his face and even his hands seemed to be touched with greenish make up. In one hand he held a lamp that burned with a blue flame and in the other he held a very large squiggly piece of metal.

"Wonder what got into her," he said.

Morris walked toward Jasmine. They heard a sound—it was music, harp music, an odd, soft chord punctuated with notes that didn't seem at first to make anything you'd call a melody. And then another leather-suited, dark-skinned figure with a big kind of squarish head showed up.

"Oh, crap," he said. "I thought you told me no one would see us."

"We're in the woods," said Botto.

"There's a baseball field right over there," said Jasmine.

"You said the door would be right here," said Motto.

"It is," said Botto. "We just have to find it."

"If we have to find it, it's not right here. If it was right here, we wouldn't have to find it. The flame would find it. Do you even know how this works?"

"Well if you'd just let me turn on the phone." The phone had the door-finder app, which could get you within several feet of the actual opening, at which point you needed the flame.

"Forget it," said Motto.

"Hello?" said Morris. "Did we become invisible?"

"Quiet," said Botto.

"Don't tell them to be quiet," said Motto. "They're humans. We're all about humans."

"I have to think," said Botto.

"If *we're* humans, what are you?" Jasmine stared at them. "And don't say elves."

"That will make it kind of hard to respond," said Motto.

"Leave them out of this," said Botto.

"What did he say?" said Morris.

"He said they're elves," said Jasmine.

"Now we tried that quadrant," Botto pointed. "I say we go this way next."

"I don't think you have any idea how to work this thing."

"Of course I do. I read all about it. Just play the harp."

Botto headed northeast, in the direction of the road, holding the lamp with the blue flame before him while Motto resumed the eerie sounding music on the harp.

"Do you think they're really elves?" said Jasmine.

"If they were elves, he'd be playing jingle bells."

Immediately Jingle Bells issued from the harp.

Botto turned around and frowned.

"They didn't think I could play it," he said. Then he turned to Jasmine and Morris. "Jingle Bells is a tad pedestrian, don't you agree?" Then he turned back to Botto, "I think we should do something about these two."

"Ah, ha," said Botto. Suddenly the flame on his lighter was burning horizontal. "Found it. He stuck the squiggly metal bar into the air. The end of it disappeared. He turned it several times. You can stop playing now. We're in."

10

IN ALL THE YEARS he'd overseen the barns no one had ever run off with a single one of Haymin's reindeer. He'd never bothered with security. He'd never had to. These were elves. And this was the North Pole. Of course elves were unpredictable, and youth was reckless—he could almost remember being young himself once— but running off with essential reindeer? That took the carrot from the snowman.

The carrot. The coal. The whole head!

Was it a sign of the times or just poor training, bad management?

What drives someone to do such a thing?

The old wood floor creaked under Haymin's heavy, fur-lined boots as he paced the barn, rubbing the upraised head of each deer as he passed until he got to the empty stalls. He stopped. He pushed his hand through the hair of his nearly bald crown and clenched his teeth and scowled. He did not turn at the sound of the big barn door sliding open behind him or at the voice of Geimle calling his name.

Geimle called his name again. "Oh, there you are," he said, approaching.

Haymin did not turn to greet him. He talked over his shoulder. "It may be time for me to shuffle off to Burzee." He stared at the empty stall.

"We'll have them back before you know it."

"For everyone there's a sign."

Geimle hand appeared on Haymin's shoulder. "Yes, there is. And we've lost more elves already this year than I care to count. But this isn't your sign. It's just two mischievous elves on a lark. You'd miss the barns too much."

Haymin finally turned to Geimle. "Doesn't mean it's not a sign," he said. "What's the Big Guy going to say?"

"Well that's what I wanted to talk to you about."

"He has to find out," said Haymin.

"Of course he does. But perhaps we wait until they're all back, safe and sound. Look better for you. Look better for me, frankly. And with him not feeling well…"

"He's no better?"

"Worse, I guess. Word is he can't even get out of bed. And you know the Big Guy. If he hears about this, he'll try to fix it, make himself even sicker."

Haymin thought it over. "I do like those two elves," he said, "generally I do. Lively pair, really."

"They're in for it, either way. But it'll be better for them too if the crisis is over before the Big Guy finds out."

"I got my report right here," Haymin tapped the pocket of his big coat.

"It's up to you when you send it, of course."

"Nothing wrong with the youth, really," said Haymin. "Could've happened in any generation. Just luck it didn't."

"It's not the people, it's the circumstances."

"I know some might've done the same thing in my day," said Haymin. "But it's still wrong."

"That may be," said Geimle.

Haymin glanced back at the empty stall. "And it doesn't mean I'm not done when it's all back to normal."

11

EVERYTHING LOOKED GRAY. And that didn't make sense. The sun was out and there were no clouds anywhere. But the sun was a big white ball like a clear full moon above the street. It was too bright and too smooth to be the moon, but it was almost dim enough to stare at.

Standing on the front lawn, straddling her bike, Jasmine squeezed the handlebars as though she were holding back an animal she expected to run away. But the ground was flat and the bike was going nowhere. In fact nothing was going anywhere. Everything around her was impossibly frozen. All the people. All the cars. Even the American flag on the mailbox looked like painted metal as it hung in a breeze that wasn't blowing.

"What the...?" Morris spun his head around looking for anything that wasn't absolutely still. It was like a wax museum or as though he were in a paused movie. But these were his streets and this was his town. He knew people who lived in this neighborhood.

What had happened? They'd entered the invisible door into which the one, the "elf" that called himself Botto, had pushed and turned the key while the other one, Motto, had bridled the other reindeer and secured two big velvet sacks to the reindeers' rumps. Morris watched the end of the key disappear in the air as though it were entering another dimension. He'd assumed it was a trick. Botto turned the key several times and then just stood there.

"You coming?"

"Absolutely," yelled Morris, grabbing his bike and running over.

"I was kind of talking to Motto," said Botto.

"I don't think you can do this," Motto said to the children.

"Why not?" said Jasmine.

"Yeah, why not?" said Botto.

"Why not?" Motto sputtered. "Oh, I don't know. Let's see: Geimle, for one. Philona. The Big Guy. I thought the whole point was to get off the planer, not take up residence."

"Yeah, I was thinking about that. I don't think it's going to be enough to show Geimle his plan won't work. I think we need an alternative plan, something that will actually solve the problem."

"Well I'm sure the Legacy Division will give us plenty of time to think one up."

"No, I think we'd better figure this out first, before we go back."

Motto huffed out a sad chuckle.

Botto turned the key several more times. "Remember, at a certain point," said Botto, "what starts as a simple transgression turns legendary. You go from being punished to being celebrated. This'll do it. I'm anticipating a parade."

"Oh, sure, with a big banner, candy-cane lettered: the first elves in the history of Christmas to sneak humans into the vortex! Who doesn't want that honor," said Motto.

But Motto didn't stop him when Botto had everyone line up side-by-side.

"Ready?" said Botto.

"Wait, wait, wait," said Motto. "Before you take the next step, remember, we ourselves have never done this before. I'm pretty sure it'll work. But if you want to back out…"

"Hell, no," said Morris.

"I'm in," said Jasmine.

"It's not exactly dangerous," said Botto.

"Maybe not *dangerous*. But we can't take any chances of getting out of sync. On the count of three, we take two steps together, at the same time, *andante*."

"That would be two steps for us, four for Dasher and Vixen," Botto interrupted. "Just being clear."

"Two walking steps," Motto resumed, "then we stop."

And then he counted like a conductor getting a song started and everyone went forward.

That's when the world went grey as the sun seemed to dip behind a storm cloud.

"Okay, we're in," said Botto. "And we're all together." And he turned around and turned the thing he called a key (which didn't look much like a key, more like the kind of crank they'd used on very old cars).

"I'm confused," said Jasmine.

"Well I expect you'll be a lot more confused pretty soon," said Motto.

The elves on reindeer led the children on bicycles through the baseball field where everyone was standing eerily still as though they were absolutely intent on the next pitch. But Morris and Jasmine didn't think much of that. It was sort of how baseball went as far as they were concerned.

"No time," said Botto as he rushed them into the neighborhood behind the field.

"I don't see how that could be true," said Motto, but they all kept moving.

And that's when they paused long enough for the freakiness to really hit. There was a man holding open the door to his car and a dog coming out of the car with one paw on the ground and one in the air and two on the back seat; it was frozen, absolutely still, like a 3D picture. There was a woman with a heavy shopping bag that she was holding by the handles standing by the trunk with her mouth open. One of the handles had broken and an orange was just falling out. It was hanging over the lip of the bag in the air as the woman's hand paused half way to grabbing it. She was going to miss.

"We're in the time vortex," said Motto.

"What the heck is a time vortex?" said Jasmine. "And why isn't anything moving?"

"Oh, everything's moving," said Botto. "It's just moving very slowly. That's why we had to all cross in together. We had to make sure we came in at the same time."

It looked like magic, but that wasn't possible. "It's not magic," Jasmine said. "There's no such thing as magic."

"No, it's not magic," said Botto.

"Not if you understand it," said Motto.

"Well, explain it," said Morris.

"It's a *time* vortex," said Botto, as though that was all the explanation anyone might need.

"What is a time vortex?" Jasmine got off her bike and walked around the car.

"A time vortex," said Botto, "is what the Big Guy uses to get his rounds done in one night. Seems like one night to you, and people come up with fancy explanations like 'time zones' and stuff. But any elementary school math student will be able to explain the flaw in that."

"You mean like Santa Claus?" said Morris.

"Yeah," said Botto, "*like* Santa Claus."

Morris didn't understand the point of the sarcasm.

"We don't exactly know how it works," said Botto.

"Excuse me, Botto. *You* don't know how it works. A time vortex—actually it's *the* time vortex, there's only one—and it's like a sleeve of time. It runs along beside regular time. So whenever you enter it the moment is synced with the moment outside it. So you have to enter it together, at least I assume you do, because anyone entering after you is on a later time stream. You'll never even see that person."

"It would be like looking into tomorrow," Botto smiled, then he looked at Motto, "I assume."

"You assume?" Jasmine waved her hand in front of the face of the woman whose spilled orange was hanging in the air.

"Well, we're not actually old enough to have done this before, as we said. It's a very high ranking thing."

"Not old enough? How old are you?"

"Almost nineteen," said Botto.

"I would have thought you were older," said Morris.

"We count in decades," said Motto.

"You're a hundred-and-ninety years old?" Jasmine's eyes grew big.

"So anyway," Motto continued, "inside the time vortex, time moves at a normal pace relative to yourself, but fast relative to the outside world as seen from the outside—which actually isn't possible because it is so fast and isn't really outside because the streams are crossed—and slow relative to the outside world seen from the inside, which actually looks like it's standing still."

"But no peeking into people's underwear drawers, if you know what I mean," said Botto.

"I don't," said Jasmine.

"Now the thing about the time vortex is that the door is always moving."

"We say it's like a snake," said Botto.

"But it's really like the jet stream, except that it moves in a more predictable pattern."

"So it's always for example at the top of the planet, if north is top—some people take issue with that, I take no stand myself—in December."

"What?" said Jasmine.

"Never mind," said Motto. "This time of year, the vortex door is in the middle of the United States, give or take."

"Actually to be specific it's precisely here, and that is why we are here. We needed to get in."

"You can pet the dog," Botto called over to Jasmine who was kneeling beside the dog with one foot out of the car. "He just won't know you're doing it."

"If you watch them long enough, you'll see movement," Motto said, "but it's like watching butter melt."

"So we can do whatever we want?" asked Morris. He was thinking about free gasoline.

"Not anything," said Botto. "There are rules of course."

"Well, not exactly rules," said Motto. "More like laws."

"I'd get arrested? Who has jurisdiction?"

Motto looked at Botto with a quizzical expression.

"Yes, I know big words," said Morris.

"Go ahead," said Motto. "Go take a piece of fruit from that grocery bag."

"Is this a sting? Are you gonna put me in jail?"

"No one's going to put you in jail," said Botto, "but we have work to do."

Morris walked over to the woman with the heavy bag and plucked the falling orange out of the air. He held it out in front to show them. "What's the big deal?"

"Now you can eat that orange, or you can let go of it. If you eat it, it will stay eaten."

"But please, don't. It's not yours," said Botto.

"But if you let go of it…."

Morris tossed it into the air. It disappeared.

"Look behind you," said Motto.

"Hey," said Jasmine. The orange was back where it had been before Morris touched it, just over the lip of the bag.

"You won't get arrested. You just can't do it. You can bring things into the vortex but you can't change things that are already here."

12

THE MAROON AND THE GREEN VELVET sacks had more things in them than they could possibly have contained. One of them was full of unwrapped gifts. The other was full of provisions, most of which was food, so it was obvious the elves intended to stay a while. They needed the food because, as Botto told them, they weren't allowed to take food from the houses.

"On Christmas Eve, people leave food for the Big Guy and his team. So that's okay. But today, no one expects us." Botto pulled something out of the red sack that looked like a rubbery pretzel. He took a bite and made a face. "Sadly, Geimle's taste in food leans heavily toward the bland."

"I think he'd say, *shelf-stable,*" said Motto.

"How long are you planning to be in this vortex anyway?" Morris asked.

"Not long," said Botto.

"A few days, maybe a week tops, measured from the outside, I'd guess," said Motto.

"Just until the gifts or the food runs out," said Botto.

"A week!" Jasmine and Morris said at the same time.

"Hard to measure time in the vortex," said Motto. "I'd say we'll have to sleep four or five times at least. Less if you help."

"Or eat half the food."

The elves assured them that they could let them out at any time, but there could be no returning if they did, as the flow of time would hurl them into the future the moment they were released, "relatively speaking."

"I thought I was starting to understand," said Morris.

"Don't try," said Botto. "Just go with it."

At first, they all went together from house to house. The elves would look around, get the lay of the land, and then deposit exactly one item, unwrapped, along with a card in an envelope in some prominent but unobtrusive spot. A lot of the things were toys, but some were decorations.

"Well that explains the Legacy Division." Motto pulled an actual "Candy Cane Express" toy train out of the bag; it was five cars long and made of sturdy wood right down to the wheels. The name was embossed on the side in traditional North Pole candy cane lettering. The Big Guy was the conductor and elves and people together were the passengers. You could take the top right off to access the detailed figurines.

"Cool." Morris pulled out the figurines to see if they were posable, then he opened the door of the box car and took out the hobo and the little banjo.

"You like that, huh?" said Botto. "You understand there's no video game tie in here? It can't talk to other trains or send crash alerts to your phone or anything."

"Oh, man, when I was a kid I would've played with this till I broke it."

"Pretty sturdy." A frown settled on Motto's face. It matched the frown that settled on Botto's face. "What are you thinking?"

"I'm a little worried."

They proceeded carefully from house to house, always stashing the one item and a little red envelope. Morris and Jasmine agreed that this would probably become quite tedious if you did it long enough, but it was anything but tedious when it was new. The stuff they were pulling out of those bags was almost always fascinating—snow globes and old cars and circus wagons and dolls and figurines from old books, and even old books in mint condition. And they also got to see and to smell every house in town. The elves forbade them to go into any of the private rooms or open any closed door, which left them mostly to kitchens and living rooms and dens and the occasional bathroom. But even so, they quickly became fascinated by how different all these houses were and then, after several dozen, at how similar they all were. Jasmine suggested they turn it into a game. Morris surprised himself by how readily he agreed. They started giving names to categories of houses. "Messy" and "neat" were the first two categories. But while the messy houses remained pretty much the same for a long time, the neat houses subdivided almost right away into "military neat" and "artsy neat," which led Jasmine to observe that *artsy* was a word that could be applied to some of the messy houses as well which led to the fourth category of "piggy." But as that ruined the symmetry of names, Morris decided that he'd rather recycle "military" but use it ironically. (Jasmine preferred the poetry of "piggy neat" as long as they were going to be ironic, but she let that go so that the game could proceed.) So they had "military neat," "artsy neat," "artsy messy," (which eventually divided into "artistic" messy, which was different from just "artsy messy") and "military messy," and "just plain messy," and then Morris decided that there was a difference between "artsy neat," and "showy neat." The categories of odors were even harder to settle upon. They worked up "sweet," and "spicy," and "funky," and "masky," and "greasy" before they decided that although the smells were closer to the personality of all these houses than the looks, they were much harder to nail down with such an imprecise vocabulary. So they skipped smells and stuck to the appearances, adding "retro," and "Wal-Mart," and "Lord & Taylor" (which replaced "showy") to the list of names before the system became hopelessly complex and they tried to think of another game.

Once Motto and Botto saw that they could be trusted to keep closed doors closed, they decided to speed up the distribution by splitting up and letting the children enter houses on their own.

"Military messy," or "artsy messy?" Jasmine reverted to the name game when they entered their own house with a snow globe for Claire.

"'Military?' not even close." That would imply there was an underlying plan the mess was obscuring. But it was just as hard to call it "artsy." "Mishmash," he said. Looking at it that way—as though he were entering someone else's house, he sensed there were two conflicting systems for order underlying the mess, his father's, which was based in the principle overlapping systems of order—one day the perfect place for the screwdriver was the workshop, the next day it was the everything drawer—and his stepmother's which was based on the principle let it fall apart until you can't stand it anymore and then clean everything. The two systems were locked in an endless and listless competition. "Mishmash messy," he said.

Jasmine knew just where she wanted to go with the gift.

13

"BREAK TIME." Botto looked around the fancy and yet informal living room of the ranch home from whose window he and Motto could look into the living room of Jasmine and Morris' house across the street. No one was home.

"You planning to spy on them?" said Motto.

"I plan to eat this freeze-dried, caramelized chicken breast with this cup of coffee." Botto pulled a thermos and a covered plate from the green velvet sack. "What rule could they possible break over there? It's their own house. Chicken?"

Motto waved off the food and stared out the bay window toward Morris and Jasmine's house. "So which one of us is going to bring it up first?" he said.

"Oh, definitely me," said Botto. "You know how I love to be first."

Motto waited. "Well?" he finally said.

Botto chewed and swallowed. "Well, before that, of course, you'll have to tell me what it is. But then I'll be sure to bring it up. You can count on it."

Motto chuckled despite his mood. "You don't see it?"

"See?" he said, "it?" And he followed Motto's gaze. "Oh, that," he said after a pause. "You're thinking that Geimle might be right after all."

"Yes."

"You mean because of the way those kids are taking to the toys. Bit of a concern. But really, out of our hands at this point. Everything else is going to plan. The hardest part's all done. I say we focus on that." Botto took another big bite out of his caramelized chicken breast.

"How can you eat like that? Aren't you worried? What if Geimle's silly plan actually works? I've got five hundred ideas I want to try out: tunable harmonicas, quarter tone pianos with double clutches, self-tuning auto harps. And what about your toy designs?"

"It's caramelized chicken." But Botto's enthusiasm seemed forced.

"It's *shelf-stable*, caramelized chicken."

Botto took another bite.

"You know," Motto went on, "I thought I was okay with the mailroom. But maybe you're right. We could have been stuck there for decades. So now that we're actually out of the mailroom—it just reminds me how I want to get into my calling."

Botto let him talk.

"I didn't think I wanted to go on this trip. But then I thought, you know, if it works, it could get us back into Geimle's good graces. Long shot, but sometimes you take a long shot."

"Is that some kind of sports analogy?"

"Trying to focus here, Botto."

"Geimle's never taken us seriously."

"But what if he's right?"

Botto put down the meat. "All right." He wiped his hands on a napkin. "I saw the human boy with the train. Geimle went all out with these gifts. I didn't realize. That boy is far too old for toy trains and even he would have played with it if he could have. I thought we might get caught. I thought we might never leave the North Pole and end up on screw fabrication or drill press operation, but I never thought if we brought this off we'd be proven wrong."

"We'll be planing boards until the sun bursts."

"We're good at our jobs, that's the problem."

"I don't think that's the problem," said Motto.

"If we'd just done our job just barely competently, passed on the requests, sent them off to the right departments, we'd have been promoted right up the chain like everyone else. But, no, we had to write back to the kids. We had to amuse ourselves and entertain them with little North Pole anecdotes and draw pictures on the envelopes. Geimle was never going to promote us."

"You don't know that."

"It's the only possibility."

"We didn't do that with *all* the letters," said Motto, "only the cleverly outlandish ones."

"It was enough. And I thought, well, if those letters we wrote didn't have any effect on people's view of Christmas, then Geimle's plan won't either. I was sure we'd show him."

"Maybe we'll get points for proving him right."

"We can't give up. And don't forget, just the caper itself is going to going to make us legendary. When we come home waving those empty sacks, there's going to be cheers and streamers. There will be poems and ballads and illustrated books."

"You're deluded, of course. You know that."

"I'm not staying on the planer *or* in the mailroom another decade."

"And if you don't get promoted, you going to join the hunt for Burzee?"

"Now why would I do that? Chicken?"

"Don't you want it?"

"It tastes like plastic."

14

CLAIRE SEEMED TO BE LAUGHING. Jasmine wished she could pull Tanya down to see it. But Tanya was upstairs standing over the sink beside a large assembly of unwashed dishes. (She had a glass in her hand into which a stream of water was hanging like rubber.) It was *that* surprising to see Claire laughing. It was an event. Claire never laughed. She was just not a gleeful person. She wasn't angry all the time either. Perhaps she was a little more likely to be angry than jolly. But she was mostly just serious—or perhaps a better word would be somber. She wasn't particularly affectionate either. But she didn't recoil if you touched her. If you hugged her, she hugged you back. Just not tightly or for very long. After a few seconds she'd say something like, "just make sure you get your homework done. I don't want to be seeing any more of those C's on your report card." But here she sat like a statue devoted to the goddess of mirth, half off her chair with her mouth contorted and eyes all squinty. At first the gesture had struck Jasmine as a frozen moment of agony. But when she looked at the whole body and, without thinking, mimicked the face with her own, it became clear that Claire was laughing.

Morris chuckled at Jasmine's mockery of Claire's face.

"What?"

"You look funny," he said.

She frowned and squished her eyes and eyebrows together. The gesture put a pause or perhaps an end to the fun he'd thought they'd been having since they'd entered the vortex.

"What's she laughing at?"

Morris pointed at the computer—at the man whose astonished face filled the screen.

"I thought she came here to work."

They could not tell much from the screen about the man who was causing this strange eruption of glee, just his name, which was Mark Tortare. The face told them only that he was laughing too, although not as intensely as Claire; his eyes were shut and his teeth were showing. They couldn't tell whether, if that face shifted back into neutral, it would be handsome or ugly.

Jasmine put the snow globe down on Claire's desk. She knew when she pulled the object from the bag that her mother would get a kick out of it. It was one of those very expensive-looking ones. It was lighted and played music. It had a wooden base and a battery compartment and a little fan so that the snow would have the energy to keep circulating—which it did until Jasmine let go. At that point it just hung in the air. Inside was a scene of the holy family—the other meaning of Christmas—but not the normal one of the babe in a manger and the cows and the wise men kneeling nearby. In this one the manger was empty except for hay, which a cow was eating. The baby was a toddler walking in front of the stable. Mary was at the window watching him toddle barefoot in the snow while Joseph with his hammer was repairing the supports to the door. The magi were in the distance on camels. And everyone had dark skin like Middle Eastern people probably would. Jasmine hadn't asked what it meant. She just knew it had Claire written all over it.

Motto told her she had to put it some place where it wouldn't just seem to magically poof into existence, somewhere out of anyone's direct vision so they could stumble upon it and wonder how it got there.

"We want them thinking about Christmas," he said, "not *Bewitched*."

But Jasmine saw her mother's laughing face and put it down on the desk right in front of Claire without thinking.

"Who is she talking to?"

"What difference does it make?" said Morris.

"She doesn't laugh like that, ever. Something's going on."

"You always this suspicious?"

"If you had my life, you'd be suspicious too."

Morris didn't think he wanted to know what that meant.

Jasmine started looking around the room for clues. There were some papers scattered on the desk, mostly pages from an article Claire was writing for a magazine. She'd printed them out and was editing them with a pen. That was not helpful. So she pulled on the drawer—which was locked. But Claire's keys were right there on top of the computer.

Morris said, "You know, when they said no peeking into underwear drawers, I think this is what they meant."

"Every rule has exceptions," Jasmine replied. "She told me that herself."

"Well maybe this is more like a law."

"If it was a law, I couldn't do it." The key turned easily in the lock. But when she pulled the key out, the drawer was still locked. "You're not gonna help?"

"What do you want to do this for anyway? So she's laughing. So what?"

"Does your dad make her that happy?"

"I have no idea."

"Do I? Does Tanya? Look, she's had three husbands. And how many stepmothers have you had?"

"Depends how you count."

"Okay, so I think we've got to be suspicious. What if she wants to run away with that clown?"

"He's just a guy on a screen."

"Is he?"

Jasmine unlocked the door again but this time did not let go of the key as she pulled the drawer open. That worked. It was a file drawer, and the first file had the word "California" written on the tab. She reached in to get it. But to do that she had to let go of the drawer, and as soon as she did that it was closed. It didn't slam closed or ease itself back into position. It just was closed. It had slipped off the key, which she still held in her hand.

"I'm gonna need three hands to do this," she said.

"You want me to help you break the law?"

"It's not a law. It's just a rule made by a guy that thinks he's an elf."

"Oh, I'm pretty sure he knows he's an elf." Morris looked around the room. "Why should I care if your mother or stepmother or whatever she is wants to run off with this new guy anyway? I told you, you'll be gone before Christmas. I know how this works."

"I care. That's why. I haven't lived in the same town two years my whole life. I want to stop that. I can't say this is the greatest place I've ever been. But it's not the worst. And I want to stay. I want to stay some place. I want to be able to say I'm from some place. I want to know if she's going to pull me away again."

"Maybe we should go ask permission."

"Since when do *you* ask permission? You're all polite to her and your father. But you do whatever you want when they're not looking. Maybe they don't know. But I do. So listen, Morris. My birth mother abandoned my father and me when I was little. I don't even remember her. And then my dad, he married Claire and then abandoned me with her. That's right: they got married and she adopted me, and then he left like he'd planned the whole thing just to get rid of me."

"Really?" Morris had not heard the details before. That was probably worse than what happened to him. He'd only lost one parent. "You remember that?"

"No. Not really. It's not clear. She told me when I was like eight or something. I should remember it. I was old enough. I was like three or four. But I don't. And now Claire, my mom, my new mom, or my second mom or whatever, has dragged me all over the country. But your dad is the first guy since then she went so far as to marry. There was Tanya's dad, and my dad, and your dad. So I thought we were finally settled. Now I just want to know how long I get to stay."

Jasmine's fists were clenched and she was trembling. Morris understood that this was the sort of situation in which you were supposed to give someone like that a hug and a calming voice, even though just a minute before they were starting to annoy you. Yes, someone needed to do that for Jasmine—but whoever that was was not him. That would just be awkward. If he tried she'd just say, "What the hell are you doing?" And he wouldn't have anything to say back. So he reached out to touch her arm and just brushed the fabric of her sleeve with the tips of his fingers and offered to hold the drawer open.

The key returned to the desk the moment Jasmine let go, but the drawer stayed open in his hand.

Inside the folder was a printout, an airline ticket to Los Angeles. Flight 150. It left in three weeks.

"There's only one," Jasmine said.

"Maybe she's going on business. Or maybe just to visit."

"You ever known her to fly anywhere on business? She does everything right here, on the internet."

"Still, she can't be running away because there's only one ticket."

She stared a moment with her mouth open. "Because she might leave me, but she wouldn't leave Tanya? Is that what you're saying?"

"No. No. I didn't say that. Look, you do not have enough information. Maybe you should just ask her?"

"Then she'll know I was in the drawer."

A voice came down the hall. "Hello, there, large human children. Anybody home?"

"Time to go," said Morris.

And then Motto was in the room with them. "Now, now, now, no drawers. We're here to deliver gifts not peek into people's private things."

"It's my mother," she said.

"No matter. If you wouldn't do that in the outside world, you can't do it in the vortex. Same rules apply."

Jasmine glanced up at Morris. Morris let go of the drawer.

15

THEY UNROLLED THEIR BLANKETS on the well-maintained lawn of a two-story home, which, thanks to the circuitous ramblings of the past couple days, turned out to be right down the street from Morris and Jasmine's house. The children were finally starting to find it more pleasant than weird to sleep on strangers' front lawns in the middle of the day.

"You can get used to almost anything," said Motto.

"Except planers," said Botto.

It was warm enough for one blanket each to suffice, which was good because Motto had—with a silencing jab at Botto—distributed the two extra top blankets they'd brought with them to the children. If there were mosquitos, they were hanging so still in the air you could see through their wings. So Morris was surprised when Jasmine said, "Maybe we could just sleep in our own beds this time. The house is right over there. I think I'd sleep better."

"Oh?" Botto had not noticed that Jasmine had had any trouble with sleeping. "What do you think Motto?" But Botto didn't wait for him to answer. "I don't see why not. Sure, go ahead."

Jasmine jumped to her feet.

"Ah, ah, ahhh," said Motto. "I see plenty of reason why not." And he told Botto about the open drawer.

"Ooooh," said Botto. "On second thought, I guess we'll all just stay together."

Jasmine put her arms on her hips: "Now, wait a minute. How are you even gonna stop me? You gonna lock me in your vortex forever?"

"Testy," said Motto. "What did we do to deserve that?"

"Oh, I would not joke about exile," Botto said, "Painful subject. I'm afraid we're just enforcing the rules. They're not our rules."

Jasmine looked over her shoulder as though she were still contemplating running.

"So, I don't get that," said Morris. "You steal reindeer and run away and take all these presents and all this food that wasn't yours, and you sneak into this vortex with us human kids, which is against your rules, but now you're these big enforcers?"

"Well, we're outlaws, of course," Botto chuckled. "Building our legend at the North Pole. Before we get back, half the polar bears above the Arctic Circle will know our names. You guys are just being sneaky."

"Like, seriously?" said Jasmine.

"There's rules and there's rules," said Motto.

"*We* are trying to make a point," said Botto. "And we're not trying not to get caught. You can be sure Geimle's hotter than a steam pipe already. We're planning on it."

"We just want to delay the actual getting caught thing until we're finished," said Motto.

"You're still stealing. You're still breaking the law," said Morris.

"We are trying to save Christmas," said Botto.

"Sounds kind of melodramatic when you put it that way," said Motto, "but you get the idea. And we're not stealing anything. We're delivering toys ahead of time—a not incidental distinction."

"And I'm trying to save my family," said Jasmine.

"Really?" Botto put down his sandwich.

"Yes, really."

"I think a statement like that earns a hearing," said Botto.

Jasmine took her hands off her hips and sat down and told them the part of the story Motto had not overheard.

"Well," said Motto when she finished. "It's not exactly a horse of a different color, but it's something."

"So can I go back to the house?"

"Probably not," said Botto.

"Definitely not," said Motto.

"Definitely not," said Botto.

Jasmine clenched her fists and tightened every muscle in her face. Botto thought she might explode.

"If we let you do that, they'll accuse us of using the vortex to manipulate human lives, which is a pretty big deal. We're not talking Geimle at this point. The Big Guy himself might be on us for that one."

"We could get exiled for real."

"But how is that different?" Morris suddenly found himself firmly on Jasmine's side of the question. He was a little surprised.

"The vortex," said Motto, "is to be used strictly for gift delivery. And that's all we're here to do. We sympathize with your plight, Jasmine. But your problem, it's an *outside the vortex* problem. Some rules are just guidelines but some are almost laws. Not even Botto would be wanting to break this one."

"Well," said Botto, "speaking for myself…"

"No!" said Motto. "The best work for an elf in this world is with the Big Guy. Wouldn't want to jeopardize that any worse than we already have."

Morris threw up his hands. Jasmine let out a big huff and threw herself back on her blanket. It was clear from the calm in Motto's voice that he wasn't going to change his mind.

The reindeer settled down at the perimeter of the circle and everyone laid back to sleep. But Motto soon sat up again. He couldn't sleep. Something was wrong; it was playing in the back of his mind. He was not sure exactly what it was or why he suddenly felt so particularly worried. Perhaps it was the unexpected tension with the children, or maybe it was the mention of exile. Morris was right as far as he was concerned. Maybe what they were doing really wasn't that different from what Jasmine had asked to do: this increasingly questionable excursion had to be tempting the exile button somewhere. Or perhaps it was still the moment of glee he'd seen in Morris when he'd picked up that Legacy train and no few other toys since then that was bothering his sleep. He needed to think. For this, he needed music. He pulled the harp out of the half-full, green sack and went behind the house to get a folding chair he'd seen back there, and he sat between the children and Botto and played soft variations on an old tune from the elven homeland that he'd learned from his parents as a child. For some reason the tune had been stuck in his head ever since he'd entered the vortex.

Everyone was sound asleep, even the reindeer. Botto smiled in his dreams as though he didn't have a care in the world. Botto didn't worry enough. It was clear his plan would not be a ringing success. If Botto had looked at the toys before he'd grabbed the bag and stolen off to the wide world, he might have known what a waste of time this was. Geimle had put more thought into his plan than either one of them had realized. He wasn't a manager for nothing. They'd underestimated him. They certainly would not be met with a parade when they got back home. And if he and Botto were already processing raw materials, what could Geimle even do to them for this that would be equal to the crime? Maybe he could send them to gather wood in the forests of Alberta. But would that even be enough? Maybe he'd have to send them all the way back to Burzee. He'd never known anyone that had happened to. But you heard stories, especially lately. Maybe they were real. Maybe that wasn't that just an expression.

Motto played the harp soft and fast. He improvised variations on the old song and hummed along with it. And then something strange happened. They were all in the middle of a large, flat, open area, but he heard an echo of the tune. That was not possible. But there it was, just for a moment, an eighth note off from every note he played. It was just a short burst, a couple of measures. He stopped playing and looked around. Everything was the same. A grasshopper hung in the air by his knee. Maybe it was a trick of his hearing. He played the tune again and on the same notes, he heard the echo again, but this time just a sixteenth note out of sync. Very strange. And he played it again and again, just that short run of four bars of the old song, an unresolved progression. And now there wasn't an echo but an amplification because the two sounds were very nearly in unison and he stood up and he turned around as he played—and there in front of him was another elf, someone he'd never seen before, very old, and not ten feet away, fingering another harp, a little bigger, playing the same tune an octave down. Motto stopped abruptly in the middle of the run and stared. The chair on which he'd been sitting disappeared. And so did the other elf, a look of surprise blazoned on his face.

16

IT WOULD NOT BE RIGHT to say the Big Guy was just another part of the problem Geimle had to deal with. Claus Ltd. was his operation after all. But still, the Big Guy was a bit—he would not want to say it too loud—just a little bit unpredictable. He might say, "Why are you bothering me with insignificant details?" Or he might hop on Blitzen and fly down to North America like a storm. He had his own way of looking at things. Elves found it baffling. Sometimes—most of the time, really—you couldn't quite reconstruct the logic. Sometimes Geimle was tempted to believe there just wasn't any. In the case of Motto and Botto, the Big Guy might blame himself. Or he might blame Motto and Botto. Or he might blame the elf who was supposed to be supervising Motto and Botto.

At least it appeared that Haymin wasn't about to run up to castle with the news.

Geimle was standing by the window in his office, looking down on the scurrying elves on second shift, when "Silent Night" shook his vest pocket. "Philona?" He put the phone to his ear.

"I'm looking right at them," she said, "locked in the case where they're supposed to be: key, flame, harp. No one's touched them."

"But Gullnle said Motto and Botto were headed for the vortex."

"Well then they're not going to get in, you can be sure. Our key is here and the original is in the vault in the castle. They won't be able to do much damage in real time. Not in the heartland of America. Sneaking around in people's houses in the middle of the night. They'll be lucky if they don't get shot."

"No need to alert the Big Guy, then?" Philona asked.

"He needs his rest," said Geimle.

17

"THE ONLY THING THAT SEEMS to move inside the vortex is the door." They were passing through the middle of the baseball field when Botto said this. The pitcher was off balance in a pose no one could hold and the batter was in mid swing with the ball just inches from the bat. Morris walked around the batter a couple times, then he plucked the ball out of the air for fun and put it in his pocket. No one said anything.

"The door should be several degrees northeast by now, I'd say," Botto continued, and he then turned to Motto, "and I still say you were dreaming."

"How could I have been dreaming, I was wide awake," said Motto.

"Because there aren't any other elves in the vortex. And you always get kind of trancey when you play music. You know you do."

"I do not," said Motto.

"Did the music go like this?" Jasmine sang a tricky tune that had been stuck in her head all morning.

"Yes, yes," said Motto, "see."

"So you were singing in your sleep," said Botto, "proves nothing."

The first sound they heard as they passed through the vortex door was the slap of a bat hitting a baseball. The bright light of the day made them squint. Morris put his hand over his empty pocket.

"You can't take anything out of the vortex unless you brought it in," said Botto. "Not even as a joke."

"That would be a law," said Motto.

"Come on, we've got to get home." Jasmine grabbed Morris' arm.

"But we haven't got the gas." Morris surprised himself more than Jasmine to hear himself say it. When they entered the vortex, he'd have given almost anything to turn around and head back home so as not to have to ride that bike clear to the gas station then all the way back. But now, after he'd been riding every day for the length of several days—he wasn't even sure how many, five? six?—a ten-mile ride seemed like hardly anything at all, like a stroll from the comfy chair to the fridge.

Jasmine looked down the road toward the gas station, still too far away to see, then back in the direction of home, over the rise, around the corner and down the road. Morris could almost see her mind working. "Never mind," he said. "Let's go home. My dad can get gas later if we still need it."

"You wouldn't happen to have a place an elf or two could hide out for a few days would you?" Botto asked.

"Huh?" said Motto.

"Well, we have to stay in the area to see how the people react to their deliveries."

"When were you going to let me in on that part of the plan?" said Motto.

"Well, how are we supposed to report back on how things went if we aren't here to see?"

18

THEY HADN'T EVEN PUT THE BIKES away when Claire opened the door to the garage. She had the fancy snow globe in her hand.

"You found it," said Morris. Jasmine hit him.

"So it *was* you," said Claire. "How did you get in my office? And where's my credit card?"

"Um," said Morris.

"Here," said Jasmine, "we didn't use it."

"We were just gonna get gas for the generator."

"So I heard. You don't use my credit card without permission, you understand? And you don't go in my office—period. I don't even know when you did that. Do you have a key?" She glared at Morris.

"No. No, I don't," he said.

Claire was having trouble processing his response. They could tell. Finally she said, "Sneaking. I do not like sneaks. I will not put up with sneaks."

"We didn't sneak," said Jasmine.

"Well, we kinda did," said Morris.

"It was a present," said Jasmine.

"And whose credit card did you buy this 'present' with?"

"Isn't it interesting?" said Morris.

"Isn't what interesting?"

"The thing," said Morris, "the snow globe."

Claire had clearly not yet looked it over. She raised it to her eyes, glanced, did a double take, and then stared for several seconds. It seemed she wanted to dislike it, but something about it held her attention. For a moment, she lost her frown. But she found it again right away. Jasmine told her to press the button to make the snow fly. But she just lowered the toy and licked her lips and looked back at Jasmine.

"I just hope you kept the receipt," she said. And she stuffed her credit card into her pocket and retreated to her office.

19

GEIMLE HAD IT WRONG, that was certain. No one's unconscious was *tickled* by these gifts. People reacted, sure, and in almost every way you could imagine, from amused to paranoid, but most by far were on the on same side of the scale as paranoia: anger, accusation, worry, fear. Most of the conversations Motto and Botto overheard were like the one between Claire and the children. Mr. Jones asked Mrs. Jones what she was trying to do, putting a Santa Claus Fisherman statue on his work bench. Mrs. Jones decided she'd pretend she knew what he was talking about, just to see what would happen. And he said, "If you don't think I spend enough time home with the family, you should just say so." And she said, "I say it all the time. You never listen." And that argument was still raging so loud it became background noise to the conversation they overheard at the Smiths, next door, where Mrs. Smith said to her children, "I'm still finding Christmas stuff in the living room. Get off your screens, get off your butts, and help me straighten up the house before your grandparents get here. You know what they'd say if they saw us like this?" She hadn't even noticed that the little diorama of a family around the tree looked a lot like her own when she was little. There was no fighting in that house, but there was a lot of grumbling. It was worse at the Spillman's. Mr. and Mrs. Spillman were the neatest couple in the whole town, maybe in the whole state. Military, Lord & Taylor neat. There was not a piece of paper unfiled in that house, not a fork that was not cradled in another fork, and not one more fork in the drawer than there were plates in the cupboard or room for at the table. When Mr. Spillman found the smiling Humpty Dumpty with the elf hat beside the pencil sharpener on his desk, he did not think of how he'd loved Mother Goose as a child, and he did not think of that Christmas long ago when his own children—now grown and gone—had given him the gold leaf, hard bound, illustrated copy of the old rhymes as their way of telling him he was going to be a grandpa (he'd kept that book on the top shelf on the left with the four other children's books that he would bring down one at a time to read his grandchildren to sleep they until they grew too old for it, and then he'd sold it and all the rest on eBay in mint condition). He saw the little figurine from the breakfast table across the room. He picked it up. He calmly called his wife. And then he called the police. And then he changed all the locks on his doors.

"I told you it wouldn't work," said Botto.

"But what about the Hendersons?" said Motto.

The Hendersons had had a fight the night before. A big one. And neither one knew how they were going to fix things up after the awful things they said. Then Judy Henderson found the Christmas bell that was engraved with the text from that movie. It was sitting on the vanity. And she didn't ask. She just went to Vincent and threw her arms around him and said "thank you" and sobbed. He never saw the bell. He didn't ask what she was thanking him for. He just hugged her and sobbed right along with her. And that was that.

"Can't win 'em all," said Botto.

Then there were the Carters. The Carters called the news. So did the Drews and the Johnsons and Sandra Lagueux.

20

NOISES AND MOSQUITOS and the thought that someone might startle you at any moment in the dark—such things can make it hard to sleep outdoors without a tent when you're no longer in the vortex. The toolshed wasn't much protection against any of them. Nonetheless, Morris met Motto and Botto that evening to unlock the door and invite the elves spend the night with the lawnmower and the garden tools.

"How is Claire?" asked Motto.

Morris made a face.

"We found her response ambiguous," said Botto, "which I guess is good."

"Good?" said Motto. "Good for whom?"

"Geimle's plan can't work if people just get confused."

They were startled by the blast of a crash that came through the open kitchen window. It was metallic, like stage thunder. Everyone jumped. The clatter was followed immediately by two voices shouting.

The first was Claire's: "I looked this thing up online. This plays music. It's got a motor. It costs over a hundred dollars. Where'd you steal a hundred dollars?"

"Why would she steal a hundred dollars to buy you a gift?" That was Tanya.

"That's what I want to know. It's not on my credit card. I checked."

"We didn't steal it."

Morris handed Motto and Botto the key. "I think I better go," and he jogged back to the house.

"I like the spunk," said Botto.

"He's going to have his head handed to him," said Motto.

CLAIRE WAS STANDING BESIDE THE COUNTER, eyes narrowed, when Morris entered the kitchen. Tanya was behind it, and Jasmine was on the floor, picking up the mess of silverware and cookie sheets.

"You don't have no hundred dollars. And what are you buying me a gift for anyway? It's not Mother's Day. It's not my birthday. It's not Christmastime. What you up to?"

"We just thought you'd like it," said Morris as soon as he got through the door. He was starting to wish they hadn't pocketed the little card that was supposed to come with it. "It was a 'welcome to the family' gift."

"See, that's nice," said Tanya. "Why have you got to be all suspicious?"

Claire looked at Morris a long time as though she was trying to decide whether he belonged in this conversation. She held the heavy snow globe in both hands. Did she want to keep it or leave on the counter or smash it on the floor with the silverware? Her eyes shifted. She was searching for words. Finally she said to Morris, "You go in my office a lot with your key?"

"He doesn't have a key," said Jasmine.

"Of course he has a key. I know he does. You couldn't get in when I wasn't there unless you had one." And then she said, as though she didn't want to say it, "What did you see in my office?"

"The door was unlocked," said Morris. "And we didn't see anything. We put the snow globe in and we left." Morris knelt down to help Jasmine.

"And we didn't steal it," said Jasmine. "We found it."

"You found it? What did it do, just fall off the back of the Christmas delivery truck?"

"It was on a garbage can," Morris said without hesitation. "Someone was putting it out with the trash. Jasmine thought of you."

Jasmine looked at Morris.

"This is a brand new condition, hundred dollar snow globe. People don't just throw away something valuable like that."

"Maybe they didn't know what they had," said Tanya.

"Of course they do," said Morris. "People throw away valuable things all the time. Some people throw away their lives. What's more valuable than that?"

Claire shot Morris a look. "What are you talking about? Who's throwing away their life?"

"People do. People throw valuable stuff away all the time because they can't be bothered." Morris picked up a cookie sheet loaded with knives and put it on the counter. "People throw away their time, their talent, their family, and all the crap they get for Christmas they don't want."

Claire put the snow globe on the counter and turned away from it. "We need to get back on topic here," she said. "Family is about trust and responsibility. It's not about sneaking around. You can't go giving presents as excuses to invade someone's privacy."

"What are you hiding in that office?" said Tanya.

"What are you talking about? I'm not hiding anything."

"Then why do you lock it?"

"Apparently I need to lock it." She tapped the snow globe with the back of her hand.

Jasmine combed the remaining silverware into a bouquet and stood it up. "She's got a guy."

"What!" Tanya stared hard at Jasmine.

"She's gonna run away. That's why she locks the door."

For a moment Claire stood frozen, like a figure in the vortex, all the muscles of her face tight, her fingers tense. She turned away from Jasmine and looked at Morris. But all she said was, "So you just put it down and walked back out, huh?"

"I have no idea what she's talking about," Morris blurted back.

"Is it true?" said Tanya.

"No, it's not true." Claire relaxed a bit. "What makes you think I'm going to do a thing like that?"

"There was a guy on the screen," said Jasmine.

"You got onto my computer? How did you…? What were you after?"

"We were just giving you the gift," said Morris. "It was just on."

"I caught you in one lie already, didn't I?" Claire looked at the window. "What was his name," she said.

Neither Jasmine nor Morris could remember. "We just glanced," said Morris.

"You just glanced? You came up with this grand theory of me running away from just a glance?"

Morris and Jasmine found it very hard to give details.

"Come with me," said Claire. "First, I'll show you this loopy story of yours isn't true. Then I'll figure out what to do about sneaking into my work space." She led them down to her office. "This the guy?" She jiggled the mouse and revealed the serious face of a goateed man, the static image of a chat screen. His name was

Willard Tremont. The text underneath the photo said, "And I might even know an agent that will help us place the manuscript."

Jasmine reached for the mouse. But Claire slapped her hand away. "He's a guy I met in a chat room for writers. We talk about publishing. That's all."

"That's all?" said Tanya.

"You gave me this snow globe so I wouldn't run away and leave you in Indiana?"

"Who said anything about leaving us?" said Jasmine.

Claire straightened up. "Now get out. I'll deal with you later. I've got work to do."

Morris said, "Well, I hope you like it, anyway."

"Free toy you picked outta someone's trash pile?" And she closed the door.

21

WTHR AIRED A STORY about mysterious "gifts" appearing in people's houses.

"What tipped everyone off was the card," said the reporter. "Each gift came with a card printed with a picture of what seems to be some imaginary workshop or other at the North Pole. The illustrations show busy, smiling elves creating the very gifts the households received. And inside," the reporter opened the card and held it to the camera, "inside it reads, 'Keep the Joy of Christmas in your heart all year.' And it's signed in big candy cane letters Geimle (elf)." She gave the name in three awkward syllables.

The camera shifted, and the reporter said a few more words and stuck her microphone under the mouth of a police sergeant. "Someone might think this was a joke." He had a nasal voice. "We do not believe it is an act of terrorism at this time. But you should know, whoever is doing this, that breaking and entering is a crime, whether you take something out of a residence or put something in. These all appear to be harmless items. But they could just as easily have been bombs."

"We're dealing with some very clever criminals here," said the reporter.

"Extremely clever and efficient," the sergeant continued. "These items are showing up all over town. This many items appearing so quickly means quite a number's involved in the distribution, possibly a gang. And this is my message to them: if you want to give away toys, do so through proper channels at the proper time. There are local charities that collect toys for Christmas. We are on the lookout. Do not, I repeat, do not enter private residences without authorization from the homeowner."

The camera panned back to the reporter. "No organization has claimed responsibility. But following on yesterday's still unexplained explosion at the Westerly substation—an explosion now officially designated as 'suspicious'—law enforcement is not taking anything lightly. I'm told there will be extra patrols on the roads tonight."

"What does she mean, 'No one has claimed responsibility?" said Motto. "He signed the cards."

"Gim-i-lee?" Botto laughed. "Who's Gim-i-lee?" And then to the TV he said, slowly, "It's GUY-mul, Geimle. Just like it says."

"Does this mean trouble?" Motto asked.

"Nah. Blow over by supper time. You watch."

But it didn't blow over. Speculation exploded: in newspapers, on blogs, on social media. People posted pictures of their gifts. Geimle (the mysterious elf) had his defenders, but most of the speculation went in the direction of street gangs or terrorists. No one managed to tie the event believably to the explosion at the substation, but the connection was never ruled out entirely. Some said the act was perpetrated by reformed thugs making restitution for their previous crimes, probably associated with some church or other, while other claimed it was the work of terrorists testing out their tactics for an all-out attack. The next time it *would* be bombs. A lot of the speculation centered on the little gift card and on the meaning of the signature. Either way, the event showed how vulnerable Middle America was. What an easy target.

Claire heard the reports in her office. They explained the snow globe, how Morris and Jasmine could have found it in the trash.

Motto and Botto, listening through open windows, collecting all the theories they could. Still, they did not know what to think. Had they really proven that Geimle's plan wouldn't work—perhaps with a little refinement? There was a lot more talk in some of these Facebook posts about the "Spirit of Christmas," than the elves had expected. And wouldn't it take time to see if this talk didn't in fact spread like some kind of happy virus? Right now the virus seemed to be favoring the negative, as you would expect from something called a virus, but you couldn't really tell who would win. In any case, clearly Botto and Motto were wrong as well. The excursion had not been neutral. The gifts had not just melted away into the general saturation of the holiday. They'd had an effect. People noticed. People were talking. This plan had legs.

On top of that, what worried them was the treatment of Geimle himself. He probably shouldn't have signed the cards with his own name. That name had spread all over the internet, where it was pulled apart and reassembled into possibilities and meanings no one would want to be associated with. They rearranged the letters and all the possibilities of sounds. They turned it into acronyms and homonyms. They explored supposed etymologies of his respectable Burzeen name, chasing down purely chance associations with human languages or the causes of angry men, and not just modern ones but even the doomed revolutionary causes from before the time of Alexander the Great. It was a little distressing.

Up at the North Pole, Geimle himself had been alerted by the surveillance office in the post office to the event and its aftermath. He followed every development from the computer in his office in the West Wing. Dismayed, he watched as his name spread from platform to platform. He watched his scheme unravel due to improper oversight. Poor planning. Poor execution. That mischievous pair had never known the details. They'd done nothing right and probably, almost certainly, they'd ruined the whole thing. On the other hand, now he knew exactly where Motto and Botto were. He was amazed they'd managed to create this much buzz in so little time without access to the vortex. (He'd checked himself: the key and the flame and the harp were safe in their case just as Philona had said.) But their failure to enter the vortex wasn't all encouraging. If they could do so much damage with so little access, well, that certainly showed how right he had been with his plan. But now that they had shown his hand, what chance was there that it would work even if it were properly executed?

He had to stop them doing further damage.

22

GEIMLE WAS UNBUCKLING THE SPIKES from his shoes when Malveno entered the barn. This time of year the short walk across the ice could be treacherous. Elves can stand the cold quite well. But slipping and falling on slick ice is another matter. It had been two months since the sun had set. And all that sunlight day and night had boosted the temperature on the polar surface above freezing. A veneer of melted ice covered every path. And today, it looked like rain—which was more than strange. It had rained once last year. But that was the only time anyone could ever remember rain falling at the North Pole.

"Seems to be getting worse every year," said Malveno rubbing his elbow as he came through the door.

"I'd think you'd use your spikes," said Geimle.

Malveno leaned his candy-striped walking poles against the wall.

"Poles have always been enough till now."

Seeing both of the wing supervisors had arrived, Haymin picked up his clipboard, drew a sad, deep breath, and shuffled over. First two rogue elves and now two high-level supervisors taking off into the wide world in the middle of the year, he'd never seen anything like it, and he'd been the supervisor of the reindeer barns since the days when he could have caught a reindeer in the wild with just his own two legs and a rope.

"Things are changing," said Geimle.

"You making a connection between misbehaving elves and the climate?" said Malveno.

"It's all related," Geimle sighed.

"But you don't see any irony here regarding your own plan for advancing Christmas into the Northern summer? I'm assuming of course that you are not in favor of the changes."

"Not all changes," said Geimle. "And as for my plan, it's more like paradox than irony. You have to do some things different sometimes in order to bring them back to the way they were. If your sleigh gets stuck in an ice melt, you may have to hitch the deer in the back to pull it out that way so you can go forward again."

Approaching the supervisors, Haymin mumbled "Come with me" and kept walking.

"Well, one thing that never changes is Haymin rules the reindeer barns." Malveno tried to elevate the mood.

"Rules?" Haymin shot back. "With all of these reindeer flying out of season?"

"Just to get the other ones back," Geimle said as the three walked the length of the barn.

"What about Fearless?" said Haymin.

"Is Fearless gone too? I thought they took Dasher and Vixen. Why would they take three reindeer?"

"They didn't. Fearless was still here after those two left. But he's gone now."

"We'll bring them back to you, safe and sound," said Motto, "if we possibly can."

"And soon," Geimle added.

Haymin's expression did not change. "And it's possible I'll still be here to stable them when you do." He stopped before the stalls of Flossie and Pacer, two of older deer, no longer used to pull the sleigh, but more than strong enough to carry a couple of independent elves.

"Possible?" Malveno said. "Not planning on retiring are you?"

"Thinking about it," said Haymin.

"Wouldn't you miss the smell of the barns?"

"Lots of us going off these days." Haymin cleared his throat again. "There comes a time for everything." Then he changed the subject as he searched his pocket for a pen. "We're still not telling the Big Guy about this I assume?"

"No need to bother him," Geimle chuckled, "sick and all. We have the authority."

"You do if I say you do." Haymin held out the clipboard and the pen to Geimle.

"Of course," said Malveno.

"Now, I haven't bothered the Big Guy, as you say, with the story of those two runaways, but…." Haymin raised his eyebrows and let the sentence hang.

"We don't want him to think we can't handle these little crises," said Geimle. "Better to tell him when it's all said and done and back to normal."

"Remains to be seen whether we can handle the crisis," said Haymin. "But as I don't need anyone thinking I can't control the comings and goings of my deer—even if I can't—sign the form."

Geimle hesitated.

"Just sign it," said Malveno.

"Of course," said Geimle. And when he'd handed it back to Haymin, he added, "No one could possibly question your handling of the barns."

Haymin yelled at a stable elf to prepare Flossie and Pacer, but then he stood by to supervise the work.

"Guess I got my wish," said Malveno, smiling when they were outside with the deer.

"We're not running away," said Geimle.

"What difference does the motivation make? We're out of school on a school day. What's better than that?"

"I don't expect it to take long. They're headed for the vortex, we can be sure of that, and they're doing some damage. But they don't have the key. I had Gully fetch the case along with the harp and the flame. They're in the sack. So they must be hanging around the area, working at night. Only possible explanation."

Malveno looked baffled. "I've never thought that part made sense. Why would they head for the vortex without the key? How could they not know how it works?"

"Oh, it's not that surprising really. Motto and Botto. Kind of self-absorbed really. And they've never yet had sleigh duties. And you know how everyone tells stories about what they don't know. They've probably heard a hundred fairy tales about how you can get into the vortex without a key. We'll clean it up—go into the vortex, collect the gifts, come back, grab the elves and haul their butts home."

"Wrap up the whole affair and stick a bow on it," said Malveno.

"Absolutely."

"You're right. That doesn't sound like fun."

23

MORRIS PLUGGED THE HDMI CABLE into the new TV. It was two days since they'd left the vortex—two days since he'd touched his Xbox. He couldn't remember the last time he'd gone two days without playing something. But he'd been busy helping Motto and Botto collect data—which really meant just eavesdropping or going around to the houses of everyone he knew and striking up conversations. Besides, he'd just been too full of going over all that had just happened to think much about shooting pixelated bad guys. Elves? Vortexes? And Jasmine. Jasmine was actually a lot of fun to hang with. That was perhaps the strangest thing of all.

But now things maybe were getting back to normal. And now he felt like playing video games again. He pushed the disc into the console and waited.

Jasmine came in carrying her guitar by the neck.

"Hey," he said.

"Hey," she said back. They sat down together on the couch. Jasmine sat right beside him. Their shoulders touched.

It was a small couch.

"You planning to play that?"

"It's not even plugged in," she said. She strummed the open strings to show him how little sound came out.

"No," he said, "I get that. I just, I haven't heard you play since the power went out."

"Look," she said, but he interrupted her.

"I know you didn't cause the power to go out."

She said she'd been trying to work out the tune that got stuck in her head, the one Motto had been playing in the vortex. It had that short melody line that had a lot of notes, but that was easy enough it pick, but she was convinced there was more of it in her head. But the more she tried to play it, the less she remembered.

Footsteps approached through the kitchen, and then Tanya was standing in the doorway, "Look at that."

"Look at what?" Morris didn't turn around. Jasmine scooched a few inches to her left. The game was just about loaded.

"You two palling around? Couple days ago I wasn't sure you even knew each other's names." And then she saw the big logo of an alien on the Titanic and she sat down in the overstuffed chair and grabbed the second game controller. "You mind?" she said. "I love this game."

Morris rolled his eyes.

"You know mom's still muttering about you thinking she was gonna run off with that guy."

"She hasn't said anything to me," said Jasmine. "But I guess it's not surprising." What *was* surprising was that she didn't seem to have told Morris' dad and that she hadn't given them extra chores or kept them from going to their friends' houses.

"You really thought she was gonna run away with that guy."

"Not like it's something new," said Jasmine.

"And abandon us?"

"There was only one ticket," said Jasmine.

"And that wasn't even the guy we saw on the screen," said Morris.

Jasmine slapped herself on the head. "It wasn't, was it? Why didn't you say something?"

"It's *your* mother," he said. "I was waiting for you."

"Whoa, whoa, whoa. What do you mean, one ticket?"

"In her drawer. We opened her drawer. She's going to California. And she's only got one ticket."

Tanya lowered the controller. "No way."

"We don't know that for sure," said Morris. "We had to close the drawer. We heard someone coming. There were other files. There could have been other tickets in the other files."

This had not occurred to Jasmine.

"Why didn't you mention this before?" said Tanya.

"It was a locked drawer," said Jasmine. "You want her to know we went into her locked drawer?"

"Why *were* you even going in a locked drawer? How'd you even get in her office?"

"What difference does that make?"

Tanya stood up. "That's crazy. Come on."

"Come on where?" said Jasmine.

"I'm going to take you down to mom's office and tell her to open the drawer and show you there aren't any airplane tickets. And then we're going to ask her where she's going and why."

"No, no, no," Jasmine grabbed Tanya's arm. "She'll know we peeked in her drawer."

"Maybe it's not a good idea," said Morris.

"Mom wouldn't abandon us."

"How do you know?"

"How do I know? I'm her daughter."

"You were your father's daughter too," said Morris. "So was Jasmine. And I'm my mother's son. So what?"

Tanya thought this over. "Well how else are we gonna know?" She took a step toward the door.

And then a voice she'd never heard before came from the other side of the room. "If I may," it said. Tanya jumped like she'd been hit. She turned in the direction of the voice, and then she jumped again.

"What the hell are you?" she said.

"The proper question would be, 'who the hell are you?' not 'what?'" he said. "I'm Botto."

Something seemed to be tugging at him from behind. He tried to slap at it without turning around. It stopped. Out stepped a similar little greenish man, frowning deeply.

"What are they?" Tanya stared at Morris and Jasmine whose lack of surprise told her they knew what was going on.

"It's 'who?'" said Motto.

"Elves," said Morris. "They're supposed to be in the shed."

"Place reeks," said Motto. "I think something died in there."

Botto waved Tanya away from the door. Motto went over and closed it, and they told her the whole story.

"I propose," said Botto when it was over, "that you let me and Motto look into that locked drawer when everyone's abed. And we'll let you know what we find in the morning."

"What happened to 'no peeking into underwear drawers?'" said Morris.

"You guys have already kind of smashed that rule," said Botto.

24

"THAT'S THEM. I SEE THEM." Gully pointed over the top of her binoculars. Karble pulled back on the reins. Indeed there was a dark spot against the clouds far ahead.

"Why you slowing down?" Prancer slowed to match Cupid's pace.

"If we can see them, they can see us," said Karble.

"Oh, yeah," said Gully. "But they don't have binoculars. And why would they look behind? They've got no reason to think they're being followed."

"How do you know they don't have binoculars?"

"Why would they have binoculars? They know where they're going. Besides, I packed their bag."

"*You* packed their bag?"

"Well, I put stuff in their bag. Did you know the key is made out of marzipan?"

"Just keep them at the edge of your sight," said Karble. "Don't get any closer."

"That," Gully suggested, "will make it a little difficult to get there first."

"We don't have to get there first. We just have to find Motto and Botto first."

"Right. How we gonna do that?"

"How should I know? Do I have to figure out everything? We'll find them when we get there."

Gully did not like that answer.

Karble had often imagined the view from a reindeer in the clouds. She'd seen pictures of course and even videos, but being here was different. Naturally, it was cold, very cold. She was almost surprised the reindeer could handle it, it was so cold. But that was of course why they used reindeer and not horses or camels. Being an elf, she didn't expect the cold to be a problem for herself. If cold were a problem, they wouldn't live where they lived. She found it bracing, the wind on her face and in her hair. The sun above the clouds is always bright. You could go right through the foulest grey day, as they had done, and then find yourself with the most perfect blue sky and the brightest yellow sun. And now they'd left even the bad weather behind. It wasn't even below them anymore, just the green of the northern forests interrupted by the tracings of rivers and the black water and the grey mountains. Just ahead big rolling clouds looked like wads of packing material.

Karble said, "You didn't have to come along, you know."

"Well if I'd known how hard it was to steal a reindeer, I probably wouldn't have. You sure they don't have footage?"

"No, they don't."

"But they're going to figure it out—two deer and two elves missing. Even Haymin can do that math."

"Yes, they're going to figure it out. You knew that. You didn't have to come," Karble repeated. "I could've done this myself."

"Yes. I noticed. You do lots of things yourself. You're putting up monitors and microphones at every corner of the North Pole, and yet I know for a fact you don't have a supervisor."

"What are you talking about? I have a supervisor. Of course I have a supervisor. Everyone has a supervisor."

"What's her name?"

Karble's face made a funny expression. She finally said, "I work out of the electronics office."

"Only that's not an office. I checked."

"What do you mean, of course it's an office. It's on the manifest isn't it?"

"It's just a room with a bunch of old junk in it. No body works there. Just you. You've been pretending you have a job when you don't. But you're doing stuff. So what's up? Where are you getting your orders?"

Karble bit her lip and brushed her long black hair away from her face. "I should have brought a map."

"What?"

"If we had a map, we could maybe plan a search strategy."

"Just use your phone," said Gullnle. But Karble said she was philosophically against using phones for maps.

"What do you mean? Phones are…. Hey, you're just trying to change the subject."

"We need to focus here."

Gullnle scratched her head and pulled on her ear. She stared at Karble a long time. "Oh, wait a minute," she exclaimed, "you were *in* maps! That's why you thought of maps. I did some work for you once. The corners of a map of Gambia."

"It was Sudan."

"That was a long time ago. So you left cartography to go rogue?"

"Left? Since when have we had an office of cartography? Who needs it? We've got these ugly, photographic, satellite-generated internet maps." Karble sounded defeated. "Satellites and cell phones. Look, yes, all right, I used to help plan the route every year. It was the best job at the North Pole. We used to track everyone, every move, every new road, every new residential construction project. We had a mess of elves doing it. It was a big job. And I was near the top. I was the office assistant for four managers. I coordinated all the finish work. I had to turn all that data into useable maps so the Big Guy didn't get lost and so he could get everything done efficiently. You can't communicate once he's in the vortex."

"It's not better than my job. Maps are just maps. Temporary. Every year you've got to have new ones. It sounds kind of little to me. I'd want a promotion."

"You didn't say that when we asked to you contribute. And they aren't little. Claus, Ltd. doesn't do anything little. I sent the Big Guy out every year with a sack of the most beautiful maps in the world. 'Beauty is functional,' that was our motto. Dorca, the head of the division, she had that printed on the wall and she said it all the time. And when a new elf said—because this happened every year—'but he just has to get there,' she would say, 'there's no "he" and there is no "there" with any "just.""'"

"And did she explain it after she said it?" Gully asked. "And just so you know, I'm still expecting this little story to circle back to the point. Don't think I'm not."

"It's a long way to the vortex," said Karble. "And, no, she did not explain it. She let it settle, which it does, eventually, if you think about it, which it will do for you too because I'm not going to explain it either."

"Hey!"

"Sometimes you don't really understand something unless the thing you need to understand just happens. Like Dorca would say, 'I can put the seed in but I can't plant the tree.'"

"She sounds like a jerk."

"Hey!"

"You don't understand it either, do you?"

"Think what you like," Karble said.

"So you're trying to make it sound all profound so I'll think you understand it. 'There's no "he" and there's no "there" if there's a "just."' Nope. Not getting it. Nothing to get."

"You're not going to get me to explain it by egging me on, so just forget it."

"That's because it's just plain nonsense."

"Do you want to hear about cartography or not?" As Karble said this, everything went white. Gully dissolved into a colorless outline. And then just as quickly she was back.

"I had no idea they flew right into clouds." Gully looked around to see if there were any more clouds in the vicinity. "What ever happened to old Dorca?"

"Gone."

"Gone? What does that mean, gone? Where'd she go?"

"I don't know. I've been trying to find out, but I think…." Karble wasn't sure she wanted to say the next part. "Look, I'm as fond of the Big Guy as anyone. He's practically kept us alive. He's given us a place to live and work to do."

"Yeah, yeah, we all know how wonderful the Big Guy is."

"They were making an atlas. It was going to be the definitive atlas. Each page was made of a flexible display screen. I helped develop it. It had the properties of paper but it was a screen. So you could set it to act like an old fashioned book. But you could also change it every year. It was revolutionary."

"Sounds kind of clumsy."

"That's what he said. They told us the Big Guy said it wasn't useful. And the managers, Geimle and the others—I think Geimle was the leader—, they all said it took up too much room. He needed his maps on a single screen that changes, not a huge book with a heavy binding."

"Sounds sensible."

"It took up less room than a sack full of maps. And it was beautiful. It was way more beautiful than those crappy NORAD maps." Karble was yelling.

"Yeah but still, one little screen versus…" Gullnle put out her palms out like the trays of a scale for emphasis.

"Dorca got mad. I don't know what else she did, but I think…. I think she was exiled."

"What?"

"There were four managers in cartography. I worked for all of them. And they're all gone. I don't know where they are. I heard them talking about Burzee. But they stopped when I came into the room."

"Karble, there is no Burzee."

"I know."

"Burzee is gone. It's a housing development in Germany."

"You don't know that."

"Or maybe Lapland. But the point is there is no Burzee anymore. You can't be exiled to Burzee, Karble. That's just a saying."

"I know."

25

GEIMLE USED HIS PHONE to locate the general area of the door. On the long flight down, he and Malveno had put together all the clues they had, from the missing sacks to the bits of information Gullnle had sprinkled into her rambling confession, and so they'd figured out more or less what Motto and Botto were up to—hitting every house in a single American town. But the plan as Geimle had developed it had never been to blanket just one town—an idea he'd rejected ("more likely to make people believe in ghosts than Christmas!"). No, his plan was to select just the right people in every town—people with lots of friends, people with a strong love for the old days, people that liked to talk—and gift them with the toys. One bag could cover half a continent. The gifts were seeds, rare and precious, to be planted carefully in the perfect soil, not common weeds you could trust to the wind.

If he and Malveno had any chance to undo the damage, they had to get the toys back and hope the ruckus would die down and the people could forget all about it. The vortex therefore was the first order of business. They'd track down the troublemakers later.

When they landed and pulled out the flame and the harp to get an absolute fix on the invisible door, they discovered the problem in their plan. Malveno strummed the harp, and it broke.

"See, I always wondered how they managed to deliver that whole load without using the vortex," he said.

Geimle sighed.

Malveno laughed.

"What are you laughing at?"

"Either at how clever they are or how stupid we are."

"I don't think stealing a key is particularly clever."

"Yeah, you're right. Stupid it is! Of course they went into the vortex. At least that mystery is solved."

"So now we have to find them just to get the key."

"They'll have delivered everything by now for certain."

"Yes, and the longer it takes us to collect it all, the more damage it will do."

Malveno took a deep breath. "I love it down here when there's no snow."

26

THAT WAS NOT MOTTO AND BOTTO staring in through the sliding glass door into the kitchen. One of them had long black hair. The other had just a thin coating of light brown hair, like fuzz. (Motto was blonde and Botto was wispy and balding.) Morris stared back, but these new elves, although they were carefully panning the room, they didn't seem to see him. He beckoned down the hallway toward Jasmine. The elves must have seen that. The fuzzy-headed one waved very excitedly at Morris and then so did the other one, who also pointed toward the lock on the door.

Morris opened the door. The two rushed in and climbed up on chairs.

"Boy, you guys get up late," said the one with black hair. "We've been standing on the deck forever."

"You guys don't seem to be worried who will see you," said Morris.

"Claire's in her office and your dad's already at work," said the other one, adding, "I'm Gully."

"Bet you thought we were Motto and Botto," said the long-haired one. "I'm Karble."

"Why would I think you were Motto and Botto?" said Morris. He didn't mention his name. He assumed they already knew it. "Where are Motto and Botto?"

"Still sleeping," said Karble. "Lugs."

"You people think we all look the same," said Gully. "Get that all the time."

Jasmine entered the kitchen, "Holy crap," she said. "More of them?"

"Pleased to meet you as well," Karble bowed without any sense of irony.

"Get that all the time too," said Gully.

Jasmine apologized and introduced herself and got herself a bowl of cereal and politely offered some to the elves, who accepted.

As they ate, Karble and Gully told them how they knew all about what was going on. They'd found Motto and Botto and got the whole story.

Having waited as long as she could, she was just about to ask the burning question when Tanya entered the room. Tanya looked at the elves, then panned to Morris and Jasmine and said, "how many of these things have you got?"

"What do you mean 'got'?" said Gully.

"What do you mean 'things'?" said Karble.

"Sorry," said Tanya.

"We went with Motto and Botto into Claire's secret lair to find out what was in those other folders," said Gully.

"We did?" said Karble.

"And did you get it?"

"We sure did," said Gully before Karble could open her mouth. "Elves are very good at getting into secret places. You were right, there *was* a second folder and there were two more tickets in the second folder. And they were round-trip tickets returning a week after leaving. Claire was going to surprise you with a vacation. And that's why she was so mad when you almost figured it out. The guy on the screen was a travel agent."

"Gullnle," said Karble loud and disapprovingly.

Jasmine clenched her fists and made a "yes" gesture.

Then Morris said, "But why would a travel agent be talking about writing?"

"Oh," said Gully, "well, that's not so unusual when you think about it. See, he's part of the whole *agent* subculture, you know, acting agents, literary agents, secret agents. It's an agent thing."

The happiness drained from Jasmine's face.

"You didn't get into the room, did you?" said Morris.

Gully sighed. "It was locked."

"That was mean," said Morris.

"Oh, I'm sure it's true," Gully lifted her bowl to drink the milk.

Just then Motto opened the door. "You guys weren't supposed to come without us," he said. And then to Morris and Jasmine he said, "We couldn't get in. Door was locked."

"I thought elves were good at getting into locked spaces."

"Well, so did Gully. And they are, I mean, we are. But first you need training. She forgot that part. We haven't had the training."

"There's a very substantial training for delivery elves. We're not delivery elves," said Gullnle. "And let me tell you, that woman has that door locked up like a fortress. She really doesn't want you going in there."

Motto cast a glance at Gully.

"So we just have to wait?" said Jasmine.

"I still think there's tickets in there," said Gully.

"Oh, maybe we don't have to wait," said Karble, and she pulled out her phone. "I've been working on this."

"She's very good with computers," said Gully.

"I went through the data base on Claire."

"We have a very extensive database at the North Pole on everyone who has ever been a child," said Gully.

"I never know when to believe her," said Morris.

"No, it's true," said Karble. "And from there I was able to hook up to her computer, which she, thankfully, never turns off."

"That's not possible," said Morris.

"No, it's not that hard," said Karble. "People think hacking is hard. It's not that hard."

At that moment they heard a scampering upon the deck. Botto banged on the door. He had reindeer behind him. "We're caught," he yelled. "We gotta go." He pointed to the sky where two objects were circling. "Geimle and Malveno."

"Not without the kids," said Gully.

There wasn't time to argue. In a moment the four elves and three children were on the backs of four reindeer running through the streets.

"And turn off that stupid phone," Motto yelled.

27

"IF WE FLY, THEY'LL SPOT US," said Motto in response to Morris' question.

"Where are we going?" Morris asked.

"Vortex," said Botto. "Only safe place right now."

"We could just fly home," Motto said.

But no one seemed to hear him.

"And why exactly are we bringing these children?" asked Motto.

"Hurry," said Gullnle, racing ahead.

The door would have moved a few dozen feet since they'd last been there. But exactly in what direction, they couldn't easily tell with the flame alone, and they didn't want to risk turning on their phones to use the door-finder app. Clearly Geimle was able to home in on Karble's signal. This would make finding the door that much harder. "I should have brought a map," said Karble, "a real one." But finding the door turned out to be less of a problem than anticipated. On the ground beside it lay the marzipan key and the broken harp and the flame that Botto had made. Dasher walked right up to them. Botto looked down, huffed, and asked Morris if he'd mind climbing down to pick them up while he scanned the area with the flame.

"Why would they do that to a work of art?" Botto muttered as Morris passed the broken replicas to Gully.

"Hardly art," she said, "though it was a nice enough job."

"They were probably angry." Motto quietly stroked the true harp. Botto's blue flame flickered as though a subtle wind from the door were blowing it—then it immediately straightened up.

"Darn," Botto said. "Louder, Motto." He held out the lit flame while Dasher slowly paced the area. "I can't get the direction."

"I'm trying to be subtle," said Motto. "Geimle's got ears like an owl."

"Yeah, but we still need to find it."

Karble and Gullnle were scanning the skies. "Oh, no," they both yelled at once.

"Have they spotted us?"

"Yes," said Gullnle. "No," said Karble.

"Phew," said Motto.

"Yes," said Karble. "Here they come."

Motto played the harp as loud as he could. The flame blew horizontal. Botto walked directly opposite the direction to which it pointed, holding the key like a sword before him until it hit the door. Morris fell to the ground as he tried to scramble back onto Dasher.

"Oh, they don't look happy," yelled Gullnle.

Geimle and Malveno tore down from the sky. Morris tried again to pull himself back onto the deer, but Dasher was not stooping.

"Well Malveno kind of does," said Karble. "He's laughing."

"Turn the key," said Motto. Botto was turning it as fast as he could.

"Stop right where you are," Geimle's voice carried from quite a distance.

"Hurry," yelled Botto. And elves and reindeer and children bolted toward the open vortex door as the forefeet of the reindeer hit the ground.

Ten steps into the vortex, Botto yelled, "hang on." And everyone stopped.

"Why are we stopping?" yelled Gullnle.

"This is far enough. We got in ahead of them. We're safe," said Botto. "They're in a different time stream. They can't catch us."

To prove it, he turned around and pointed at the open door where, in a bright patch of light, they could see Geimle and Malveno landing, simultaneously, the rear ends of Malveno's reindeer still in the air.

"Safe," he said again.

"What happened to the sun?" Tanya had been sitting on the rear end of Cupid in back of Karble all this time in pretty deep confusion. She'd watched one elf playing a harp and other roaming around with a lighter like an old cigarette lighter and then the first one turning a metal rod in the air like a mime cranking a Motel-T. And then all the deer bolted like crazy and then they stopped before they even got up to speed like they didn't really want to get away from the other elves who were chasing them but who didn't follow. And now they were acting like they were somewhere else even though they were still in the woods and nothing was different except the sudden dimming of the sun.

"Where's Morris?" said Jasmine. She yelled his name.

"Someone tell me why we brought these children with us?" said Motto.

"He fell down," said Botto, pointing again at the sunny patch through the open door. Jasmine hadn't noticed him there, on the ground between the descending reindeer.

28

"SEE," SAID TANYA. And she took a step toward Morris, but then paused in front of the reindeer, suspended as though they were encased in the air like a bug in a glass cube. But there was no cube. He was just there. Morris was part way to his feet in almost like the pose of a sprinter waiting for the gun to go off or like someone in a very weird yoga position, with his hands off the ground. Nobody could hold that pose. "What the hell's going on?"

"Don't touch him," Gully shouted. Jasmine pulled back her hand. "He'd fall over," Gully went on.

"No, he wouldn't," said Motto. "Things just go back to how they were. How many times have we seen that?"

"No, he would," Gully said back. "He'd fall right over. Look at him."

"He would?" said Botto.

"Yeah, there's all sorts of stories about elves using the vortex to play tricks on people before the Big Guy got the key."

"You seem to know a lot about the vortex," said Motto. "Why didn't we take her with us to begin with?"

Gullnle rolled her eyes and planted her face in her hands.

They'd circled back to the door. But they went around it instead of through it. They were right there with Morris and the two new elves, but Tanya and Jasmine and company were still inside the vortex while Geimle, Malveno and Morris were out. Much debate led Jasmine and the elves to conclude that Morris would enter the vortex at just about point at which the elves could catch him.

"Could take a couple days," said Botto, "relatively speaking."

"But what if they don't enter together?"

Their own mad dash to the door revealed that a second just at the door, where time was collapsing to create the breeze that moved the blue flame—just there that second or so didn't seem to matter. They hadn't all crossed the threshold in lock step, but they'd all made it together. So these three would probably enter in on the same time stream.

"And then they'll boot him out and lock the door," said Botto. "We can say goodbye to Morris."

"Speaking of which," said Motto, "now that we're safe inside the vortex, I think it's time we answered a couple of questions." He stood up on his reindeer.

"Go ahead," said Gully.

"First of all, what's the plan?"

"The plan was to escape Geimle and Malveno's wrath," said Botto.

"Wrath?" said Karble.

"You ever worked on a planer?" said Botto.

"And what's the second question?" asked Gully.

"Why did we bring these children?"

"Oh, that's easy. We want to figure out what's going on with Claire."

"Really?" said Motto.

"Oh, sure," said Karble. "We talked about it, me and Gully. Fascinating story."

"Besides, maybe we can help," said Gully.

"But that's not what we do," said Botto. "We're kind of all about presents. We're not supposed to help people."

"Well," said Karble, "it's not what we did. But we're here. And we're stuck. And unless you want to run right back into these guys," she slapped Flossie's rump, "might as well see what we can see."

"You thought we were just going to sneak in and wait for the coast to clear then head back to the North Pole?"

"Pretty sure that's what I'm still thinking," said Motto.

"Not gonna happen," said Gully.

"Well, we're stuck in here for a couple days, anyway," said Botto.

Motto sat back down on Vixen and scratched his head.

29

"HANG ON THERE, HUMAN CHILD. No people allowed in the vortex."

Morris jumped to his feet and ran in the direction of the subtle shift in color that showed him where the open door was. The two elves and their two deer dashed after him, catching him just as he crossed the threshold.

Geimle jumped off his mount and put his hand on the boy's shoulder.

"We do have to enforce the rules."

"Jasmine," Morris yelled. And he pushed the elf's hand away.

"We'll find your friend," said Geimle. "But you have to leave."

"I've already spent days and days in here. I know all about it."

"Doesn't change the rules," said Malveno, climbing down. Morris was taller than either of these elves, but they were solid. He could tell from the grip of Geimle's hand on his shoulder that they would have no problem wrestling him back through the door if it came to that.

"Well, look at you, come to your senses," Geimle said to Malveno.

"There's rules and there's rules," said Malveno as seriously as Geimle had ever heard him. "And we have to close the door."

"Good luck with that," Morris dashed off in the direction of the ballfield.

"Does he think he can outrun a deer?" said Geimle calmly.

Geimle remounted Flossie and gave chase while Malveno wound the key to close the door.

Morris didn't have to outrun the deer. He just had to get a certain distance from the door before the deer caught him. He dodged trees to make it harder for the deer to follow. He jumped the fence around the baseball field—which even as he did it he realized he probably couldn't have done just a few weeks ago—and he took off for home plate. When he got there, just before Geimle, whose reindeer leapt the fence with ease and tore after him, he sat down and folded him arms.

"Not going," Morris said when the elf arrived. "I know how this place works, and I'm going to find Jasmine. And I'm going to help her."

Geimle tried to explain the problem. Malveno arrived and tried to reason with him.

"One question," said Morris, "do you really think you can pick me up and carry me all the way to that door? I won't made it easy."

"That would be a lot of work," Geimle said.

"I know all about the vortex. I know where they're going. I can help you find them."

The two elves looked at each other. Geimle measured the distance to the door.

30

"FIRST THINGS FIRST," said Botto. "Collect the toys."

"What?" Jasmine almost fell off her reindeer. "What about going home and finding out if my mom is planning to abandon us?"

"There will be plenty of time for that. We're in the vortex," said Botto. "There's time for everything."

Then Motto told the children what Karble had told him: that Geimle had never intended to blanket the whole town and that he was coming here to undo their work.

"Well, then why not just let him?" said Jasmine.

"We talked about that," said Motto.

"And we decided," said Botto, "that really we've already proven as much as we could prove. And since our point has been thoroughly and irrefutably made, we might be able to take the edge of Geimle's snit by saving him the trouble of having to look for all the loot. We have a much better idea of where everything is."

Motto smiled and slapped his friend on the back.

"Don't forget I also said you might want to apologize too," said Karble.

Botto shrugged. "Maybe," he said to Karble. "But that doesn't mean we were wrong. We weren't wrong. They won't be *real* apologies. Geimle's plan was doomed. It wasn't going to work. And we proved it. I say we proved it."

"In that case maybe you should offer to wash Geimle's marble floor as well," added Gullnle.

In the process of collecting the toys, Motto told the children they'd work their way to their house and see what they could do about Claire from the inside.

During the conversation Tanya caught Jasmine's eye and shook her head, mouthing something the elves didn't see.

Jasmine nodded at Tanya.

Tanya said, "Me and Jasmine are going home." She slipped off Vixen and started walking. Jasmine dropped herself off Cupid and followed. She said, "just make sure you don't leave without us. We'll be at the house when you get there."

"Hey," said Gullnle.

"They don't work for us," said Karble.

"That'll slow us down," said Motto.

"There's no rush," said Gullnle.

"Everyone keeps leaving," said Botto. "You know we've got elves leaving the pole and that slows us down and now these kids leaving us."

"You don't think those are related?" said Karble.

"I just think the real solution to everything is for the Big Guy to get better. He would've stopped Geimle from ever making his stupid plan and then we never would've been put on the planer and then…."

"Not so simple," said Gullnle.

"Perfectly simple," said Botto.

"Oh, I'm sure Botto's right," said Karble. "The Big Guy will be fine soon and everything will be back to normal and we can forget the whole thing."

"Why do you think that?" said Gully.

"I just do."

"You don't know something you're not telling us by any chance?" Gully asked.

"Of course not."

"Hmmm." Gully paused and waited for the others to jump in. But they didn't. "Okay. Well, so listen—there's a few things I think you guys need to know. I wasn't going to say, but the truth is, I happen to know what's really going on."

"Oh, you do?" said Karble.

"And it's not what you think." Gully gathered the four of them around the kitchen table of the first house on the block, maneuvering past two humans who seemed to be entangled in an argument or heated discussion over the kitchen counter. A woman on one side of the counter was in the process of cutting a melon, the two halves of which were lying with their exposed seeds while she was pointing emphatically with her knife at another woman across from her. That woman had her hands in the air in a "who, me?" pose. In between them, beside the melon, was a toy, one of Geimle's toys, a wind up monkey with cymbals and a drum. Motto grabbed it and put it in the bag.

"Well, that one was a dud," he said.

"You don't know," said Botto.

Gullnle took the knife from the woman's hand and finished cutting the melon.

"You can't eat that," said Motto.

"Why not?"

"It's not ours."

"*Elves*," she said.

"And?" said Botto.

"Do you think the Big Guy lives off cookies and carrots?"

"Well then why did Geimle have that big bag of food?"

"Maybe he doesn't like human food," Gully supposed.

"Really?" Botto remained doubtful, but he accepted a slice of melon. Gully let go of the knife, which returned promptly the hand of the irate woman.

"Of course. Elves take stuff all the time. Why do you think they call us mischievous?" Gully distributed the rest of the melon.

"So what's the story, Gully?" Karble sounded suspicious.

"Listen, listen," she said, "Geimle's plan, it was never what he said it was."

"Oh?" said Karble.

"I've been doing some investigating. I've been doing a lot of investigating. It's still kind of incomplete because I can't get into the castle. But I'm pretty sure, in fact I'm positive, something's very, very, *very* wrong. I don't think the Big Guy's in charge any more."

"What?" said Motto.

"Well not while he's sick," said Karble.

"No, I mean at all. Is he really just sick? I don't think so. Everyone's saying he's just a little under the weather. But it's not that. No one's 'a little under the weather' for most of a year. No, he's not making *any* decisions. Because he can't. I don't even think he's at the North Pole anymore."

"How do you know this?" said Karble.

"You might think maybe he doesn't want to, maybe he's given up. Maybe he's discouraged or just old. People do get old you know. But what if he's just plain gone?"

"Geimle!" said Botto.

"Well, not exactly," said Gullnle. "Only, listen, the thing is, it's worse than you imagine. We're losing elves. You know that. And not just in cartography either. But why are we losing them. *You* think they're going away. *I* think they're being sent away."

"Exiled," said Botto. "Ooooww, that Geimle."

"No," said Karble.

"If the Big Guy's not in charge, who's sending them away?" asked Motto.

Everyone was silent.

"Gotta be Geimle," said Botto.

"Bottom line: we're going public," said Gullnle.

"Okay. That's just ridiculous," said Karble.

"No, no, no, everything fits," said Gullnle.

"It kinda does," said Motto.

Karble grabbed her long hair in her fists and pulled.

"Except for the going public part," said Motto.

"Well that's just it," Gully's voice rose. "Geimle's taking over. This plan was just the beginning of his coup. He's going to streamline. He's going to redefine the whole operation. And he isn't going to need so many of us."

Motto took a last bite of his melon and set the rind on the table. The rind just sat there. He picked it up and dropped it several times as though he found it suddenly more interesting than what Gullnle was saying.

"Didn't you notice," Gullnle went on, "any time anyone gets wind of what's really going on, they get whooshed away, or they bolt on their own—one or two at a time, so maybe everyone sees, but no one really notices."

"The Big Guy would stop that, even if he was sick," said Botto.

"So that just proves it, there *is* no Big Guy any more. Maybe he was fired. Maybe he just left on his own like the elves."

"Without saying goodbye?" said Karble.

"So that's why Geimle's so fired up about this plan. It was supposed to be the launch of the Geimle Christmas Empire."

Karble could hold in her consternation no longer. "I happen to know that that is *not* true."

Gullnle gave her a kind of sly look, "Oh?" she said, "And how do you *know* that?"

"I just do," she said.

"Well I for one don't believe you," said Gullnle. "Who's got the better story? *I* have facts. *She's* just saying. When was the last time any of you actually saw the Big Guy?"

"Christmas," said Botto.

"In a sleigh, from a distance? That could've been anyone."

"No. He was there for the celebration just like always," said Karble.

"If *you* say so," said Gullnle.

Motto picked up the melon rind and squeezed it.

"But we have to act like we don't know about any of this," said Gullnle. "Because otherwise, we get the boot."

"Oh, I think we've all done enough already for the boot if there was any booting to be got," said Motto.

"I've been trying to act like everything's normal for months," said Gullnle, "like I didn't know anything because everyone who finds out—it's just 'zoom, out of here.'"

Motto dropped the melon rind on the table again. "Why doesn't it go back?" he said. "Why does it stay here? I'm not touching it."

"Well you changed it, of course," said Gullnle as though melon rind had been the subject all along. "You ate it. You brought it into our time."

"I didn't eat the rind."

"Don't you know anything about the vortex?"

Motto had thought he knew all he needed to know. But then there was the elf who'd appeared the last time he was here when he'd played the harp. "We should have studied up on the vortex a little more," he said to Botto.

"I say learn what you need to know and then stop or you'll just get confused," Botto replied.

"I think we've straying from the subject here," said Gullnle.

"I think we're done with that subject," said Karble.

"Prove to me I'm wrong," said Gullnle.

"I don't have to," said Karble. "You just are."

Gullnle gave her head a flustered shake.

31

JASMINE WENT STRAIGHT to Claire's office. It was locked. Claire was inside. It was the middle of the day. But she'd locked the door.

"That's weird," said Tanya.

"Almost paranoid," said Jasmine.

"It doesn't mean she's running away. She wouldn't just run away from…" and then she paused before adding "us."

"We've gotta get in," said Jasmine.

The girls had to figure out how to do that. There was no reason to rush anything when you were in the vortex. They went upstairs to think about it. Jasmine picked up her guitar. "Should we break the door?" She had already shown Tanya how things always went back to their previous place when you let them go. When she laid her guitar down for a second, she had to chase it back to the den. So even if they broke the door, she said, it would go back together as soon as they got in the room. Of course then they'd have to break it again to get out.

Jasmine said she'd go out to the garage for the sledge hammer.

But Tanya didn't like any part of that idea. Something was bound to go wrong. And there was a little struggle before she said, "We've got elves. Let's just wait and see what they say."

Jasmine wasn't encouraged. "The elves already didn't make it into that room once."

"But that was outside this vortex thing," said Tanya.

Jasmine couldn't see how that could matter.

"Motto and Botto are all against us sneaking around like we're trying to do."

"Yeah, but the other two seem to be in charge. And they said they want to help."

Jasmine strummed her guitar. "But what if…"

"I don't know," Tanya said. And *you* don't know either. So we'll just wait and see. We're not going to hammer down a door."

Jasmine and Tanya were settling in for their third sleep when the elves arrived at the house—at last and, despite how time moved in the vortex, just in time. They were three pretty boring days most of the time for the sisters, with odd spikes of anxiety during which Jasmine threatened to smash the door. Tanya wasn't sure how long she would be able to hold her off. There wasn't a lot to do. They read a lot of books. Jasmine played her guitar a lot. Tanya sang. They tried to play games, but that proved impossible because you could never let go of the pieces. This must have been what life was like before the invention of electricity, they thought, but with less to do. Electronics didn't work at all. Books worked just fine. Tanya spent most of her time reading. Jasmine found herself obsessed with that elven tune that had got stuck in her head. She figured a lot of it out. But there were still measures missing. She'd have to ask Motto about them after they got into Claire's office.

Jasmine and Tanya rushed the four elves right down when they arrived.

Motto tried the door even though they'd already told him it was locked. "Any other way in?"

"There's a window. Also locked," said Tanya.

"Can't you just break it?" said Jasmine.

"Broken stays broken," said Motto. "I learned that."

"Are you saying we've stayed here for all this time waiting for you and you aren't going to do anything?" Tanya said.

"Yeah, kinda," said Botto. "Got any food?"

Jasmine's face dropped. "I'm gonna break the door." She started up the stairs.

Gully called after her: "We're not giving up that easy. I've got a plan."

Gully gathered everyone in the living room. Jasmine brought her guitar.

"Okay, so my plan is this. We brainstorm on our situation and come up with definite, specific lists of all the possibilities, then we vote on the most likely and do that."

"That's a plan?" said Karble.

"There's not that many variables," said Motto. "Locked door, locked window. I don't suppose there are air ducts like in the movies?"

"So we're just going to stop helping these girls find out what's going on with their mother?" said Gully. "I do not think so."

"Well, you know, we tried." Motto looked relieved.

Karble strolled over to Motto and looked him in the eye and smiled. Motto smiled back. "No, we didn't," she said. And she tweaked his ear. And then she spun around and smiled at Tanya, "We're gonna figure this out."

"That's the spirit," said Botto.

"There's certainly a way," said Gullnle.

"Not necessarily," said Motto. "There isn't always a way. And Geimle…"

"There's got to be a way," said Gullnle.

They sat around the living room for a long time not saying very much. If there was a way, it clearly wasn't going to slip down the Chimney and introduce itself.

Jasmine let her fingers rush through the tune as the elves tried to come up with a way forward. It was a slow discussion with a lot of hemming and hawing. The question soon turned to whether they had exhausted all the in-vortex possibilities and had to try again from the outside.

Apropos of nothing, Gully turned to Jasmine who was fiddling with her guitar. "Where'd you learn the gathering song?" she said.

"She's nearly got it down too," Motto said. And then he complimented her.

It was starting to look more and more as though they'd met a dead end with Claire, but maybe the music would make everyone feel better for a little while. Motto retrieved the harp from the sack and slowly played the parts of the melody Jasmine was still vague on so she could copy him. It was a tough little sequence, but she was a quick study. Soon everyone put the question of Claire to the side and relaxed to listen to the two musicians riff off the clever tune. A harp and a guitar. And then another harp, kind of plunky. Gully had pulled a harp that had been given as a toy from the sack and joined in. The tune went on and on and got louder and louder. Tanya wanted to know if there were words. So Botto and Karble and Gully started to sing. Tanya learned the sounds. She didn't understand them as words—they were in the Burzee dialect of a particular elven language—but she picked up the sounds and sang along with the others, over and over. It was the kind of jaunty tune you could sing like a round.

And then a harmonica joined in.

Who had a harmonica?

Jasmine stopped strumming. Motto stopped plucking. The singers went silent—except for Gully. Gully kept right on going, her eyes closed. She was riffing and laughing—until Botto put his hand on her strings to stop them vibrating.

"Hey," she said, opening her eyes.

The harmonica kept playing.

And there in the middle of the room stood Malveno and his E-flat harmonica. Morris had his hand on his left shoulder. Geimle had his hand on his right.

Geimle didn't look happy.

"Oh," said Gully. She knew what had happened. She probably should have said something about it. Her eyes darted around the room. "Look, Geimle, we caught them!" she said, "me and Karble."

"We did?" said Karble.

"We did!" said Gullnle. "And we tricked them into playing the gathering song."

"We did?" said Karble.

"You boys didn't remember about the Time Vortex Gathering Song that you play every Christmas when you enter the vortex to get all the native elves to sync up for delivery." She turned to Geimle, "Thank goodness you knew we were doing it so you could play your harmonica. I was afraid you weren't going to join us."

Karble stared disapprovingly.

"We heard the harp," said Malveno. "Pretty easy from there."

Motto looked at the harp on his lap as though it were something he'd never seen before: an instrument that could send waves through vortex time.

"Hey, Geimle," said Botto.

"So what do we do now," said Gullnle, "now that we've caught 'em?"

"Now we finish gathering the toys and head back home," said Geimle. "I have some choice jobs for which I still have to assign young, capable, ambitious elves."

"Oh," said Motto.

Tanya and Jasmine stared mutely. Tanya was about to say something, but Jasmine put up her hand to keep her quiet.

"The snow globe is in Claire's office," she said, "downstairs. I'll take you." She got up and started toward the stairs, but Malveno called her to him by name. She didn't like him using her name. It felt wrong for someone who should not know your name to use it. She hesitated.

"You don't have to be afraid of me," said Malveno in his musical voice.

"You don't," said Morris. "They're actually very nice."

She still hesitated until Botto himself said without irony, "Yeah, that's actually true, Jasmine."

"Isn't he the one you're always complaining about?" she whispered.

"I was afraid she'd say something like that," said Motto.

"Actually, that's the other one," said Botto. "But he's nice too, really." Then he turned to his boss, "We never said you weren't nice. Only…"

"I don't need to know," said Geimle.

Jasmine whispered to Karble, "But aren't they the bad guys?"

Gullnle looked at Jasmine, "Hey, you know the story. You're a child; they're elves. That job stuff, that's just among us. They work for the Big Guy. 'Nice,' is kind of a job qualification. I mean, c'mon. They're elves. We're all elves. We don't do 'bad guy.'"

Jasmine let down her guard. Malveno beckoned her like a shopping mall elf would do. He said, "Morris told us what this is all about."

She cast a distrustful look at her stepbrother.

"I was trying to help," he said.

"And he *was* helping," said Geimle.

"But here's the problem," said Malveno. "We're not supposed to mess around with your personal lives. If we started doing things like that, we'd never do anything else, and we'd never get to the end. People have to work out their own problems. That's a very basic elf rule."

"You give us toys. What about that?" Tanya said.

"Yes, we do. Under certain conditions, we do that. But that's all we do. We give you gifts. And we want the gifts to make you happy. We spread goodwill. We think it's useful."

"We hope it's useful," said Geimle.

"We're kind of having a debate about that right now, up at the North Pole. It's kind of what this whole thing has been all about," said Motto.

"I don't know if there is a real problem between you and your mother," Malveno said. "Maybe there is. And if there is, I really hope you can fix it. But we don't have the knowledge or the authority or the expertise."

"We'd either create a problem that doesn't exist or we'd make a real problem worse," said Geimle. "Right now, we have to take you home, out of the vortex. And we have to get these other elves back where they belong. I'm sorry."

"You're sad." Malveno reached out to her to draw her closer, but she didn't move. He brought back his arm. "But you're not in any real danger. And you don't belong in the vortex."

"Just for the record," said Botto, "I think that stinks."

"You're in enough trouble." Geimle glared at Botto. Botto shrugged.

Malveno told the children to stay where they were. He took Motto downstairs to help him find the toy.

"The door's locked," said Motto.

Malveno pulled a little card out of his pocket and slipped it between the door and the casement just beside the door knob. The door opened easily.

Motto saw the toy first. It was right there on Claire's desk beside a pile of notes and Claire's credit card. He put himself between Malveno and the toy and glanced into the back corner of the room. "Why don't you try over there," he said. Malveno glanced in that direction.

"No, no. Here it is," Motto said. And he picked up the globe and palmed the credit card.

32

THE CHILDREN DOUBLED UP behind Malveno and Geimle and Karble. Motto, Botto, and Gullnle lagged behind with the whole stash of Geimle's prototypes. They were doing a lot of whispering.

Geimle looked over his shoulder: "I wouldn't be planning any new escapades to get yourselves off the planer."

"Oh, no," said Botto. "We've learned our lesson."

"Very good." Geimle paused until it seemed he'd said all was going to. Then he added, "because it may be a while before you move back up to the planer."

"As long as you don't exile us," Botto joked.

Geimle stopped. He turned Flossie around and looked very serious. Everyone stopped and stared at the senior elf.

"Excuse me?" said Geimle.

"Just a joke," said Botto.

"No one's being exiled." He was deadly stern.

"I know, I know, ha, ha. Little joke."

Geimle stared at Botto several long seconds. "No one's being exiled," he repeated. He looked at each of the elves from face to face. No one knew what to say. Not even Gully. No one was tempted to make a joke. But if anyone had, looking back at Geimle's hard eyes, no one would have laughed. Without another word, the boss turned Flossie back toward the vortex door.

Malveno put the key in and opened the door wide. "We have to leave together," he said, and the six reindeer lined up in two rows. Geimle gave the command. He and Malveno and Karble and the children stepped forward. The moment they did, Motto, Botto, and Gullnle took half a step forward, then turned around and fled together into the vortex as fast as their deer could fly.

"Unbelieveable," said Geimle.

"You must not know them very well," said Karble.

Malveno laughed. "I have to say, I love those elves."

Geimle didn't laugh. But he was finding it hard hold onto the stern rebuke of the moment before. Maybe it was the southern air or, as Malveno had said, being out of school on a school day, or maybe it was just being around human children—and not scared or bug-eyed children, but just regular human kids. Despite himself, he was finding this adventure just a little bit entertaining. "They do realize they're going to be stuck, of course," he said. "They don't have the key and we can't leave the door open."

"I doubt they thought that far ahead," said Malveno.

Karble frowned.

"Maybe we'll find them again at Christmas," said Malveno.

"They have my toys," said Geimle.

Sticking to the woods as much as they could, they took the children within a mile of home before they parted. The children walked the rest of the way home. The elves took off several feet from the road and headed back to the Pole.

33

MORRIS HELD THE DOOR OPEN as Tanya climbed the stairs. Jasmine was already inside.

"Enough exercise for one day," Tanya said. Morris almost laughed. They both heard Jasmine's call of surprise from the family room.

Morris and Tanya rushed in to find—somehow—Motto and Botto and Gullnle sitting side by side on the couch, each with a game controller in hand, guiding virtual cars through the streets of New York. Botto had a beard, which he had not had when they left him at the vortex just a little while ago. They had a large sack of toys at their feet.

"How'd you…?" said Tanya.

"Where'd you…?" said Morris.

"Aren't you afraid someone'll see you?" said Jasmine.

"Elves," said Motto, as though that answered all three questions.

"Been waiting for you," said Gullnle.

"How's *that* possible?" said Tanya.

Motto turned off the game.

"Hey, I was winning," said Gullnle.

"No you weren't," said Botto.

"I was almost winning. I had a strategy," said Gullnle. "Where have you been?"

"How'd you get out of the vortex?" said Jasmine. "You went the other way."

"It's a *time* vortex," said Botto. "We were in it for months."

"And we made a key," said Motto and he pulled the oddly shaped metal bar out of the bag of toys sitting beside the couch. "Botto had an exact marzipan copy. So—we just copied the copy."

"But how'd you get here before us?" said Morris.

"You walked. We flew. It's not that hard," said Botto.

"Don't you want to hear about our investigation?" said Gully.

"What?" said Jasmine.

"We did some digging," said Gullnle. The kids sat down. "We think your mother's a spy."

"No, we don't," Botto exclaimed. "Where did you get that?" He scratched his head.

"Oh, I've been working it out," said Gully.

"Let me tell it," said Motto. Gullnle frowned and Botto rolled his eyes, but they let him tell it. "We went back into her office."

"How'd you get in?" said Morris.

"The old credit card trick," Botto explained. "Motto saw how Malveno jimmied the lock."

"But *she* said it was locked up like a fortress," Jasmine pointed to Gully.

"Who knew?" said Gully.

"Oh, that reminds me. You better give this back," said Motto, handing Jasmine her mother's scratched credit card. "No, there are no more tickets in that drawer. But there are paper files on both of the men you guys saw on the screen."

"At least they better be those guys, or we wasted a lot of time," said Botto.

"Mark Tortare and Willard Tremont," said Motto. "She had their names and addresses in another folder in the drawer with the tickets. So we chased them down."

"What does that mean?"

"We went to California, obviously," said Gully.

"Time vortex," said Botto.

Motto went on. "Willard Tremont is single. He teaches math at a community college in Buena Vista, lives alone. Writes fantasy and mystery stories that use a lot of math."

"And they're not very good," said Botto. "Fan fic mostly."

"He seems to spend most of his free time on the internet, trolling for friends, playing with math and looking for publishers."

"Okay," said Jasmine. It was hard for her to see what Claire would see in him.

"Mark Tortare is single. He has a nice house in Yorba Linda. He's a lawyer with two children."

"And?" said Tanya.

"That's all we found out," said Motto. "Everything else is online. You can't use computers in the vortex."

"So you've got nothing?"

"We hoped it would mean something to you," said Botto.

The children couldn't imagine how.

"Well there's a pack of weeks I'll never get back," said Gully.

"What now?" said Jasmine.

"Now we go home," said Motto. "We're in a snowpack of trouble as it is."

"Up to our necks and over our ears," said Gully.

Footsteps came up from the cellar stairs. Claire called Jasmine's name then Tanya's.

Before the girls could say "in here," the elves had dived out of sight, taking the bag of toys with them. Morris shook his head in amazement. Then Claire was in the doorway, smiling. She stepped in. "Listen girls, I have to go away for a few days."

"Go away?" said Tanya.

"Yeah Willard, the guy who said he could help me," she talked very slowly, "he's set me up a meeting with a agent. I need to... Is that my credit card?" Jasmine handed it over. "Again? You took my credit card again?"

"I just found it. I picked it up. It was on the table. I was going to give it back to you."

"It was not on the... It was... It was..." She looked back in the direction of the stairs. "Why would I leave it on the table?"

"What do you mean? You leave things lying around all the time. It was just on the table," said Tanya.

Claire plucked the credit card out of Jasmine's hand.

"We just found it." Tanya was trying to stay calm.

"When are you coming back?" said Jasmine.

"Couple of days. It all depends, really." Claire stared at the credit card in her hand. "You didn't happen to see that snow globe when you found this credit card?"

"Why?" said Tanya.

"It's missing, of course. That's why. I put it right on my desk."

"We didn't go back into your office," said Morris.

"I know that. I just. I was sure..."

Jasmine heard a little scratching sound on the floor and looked down at her feet.

"Actually, it's right here," said Jasmine. "They were together on the table." She picked it up. "Do you want it?"

Claire stared at each of the children a moment before reaching for the snow globe. "And none of you is suppose to be playing that game. You turn that off. I don't know why your father lets that stuff in the house."

142

"She's nervous," said Jasmine when Claire was too far away to hear.

"How do you know?"

"That's how she talks when she's nervous."

"Or angry," said Tanya.

Claire kissed her daughters at the door and gave Morris a hug when the cab arrived to take her to the airport.

34

THE WORD CAME DOWN from the castle in unsigned reports over the North Pole intranet. Everyone got it. No one could figure it out. The Big Guy's health had taken a turn for the worse. (But what did that mean? Fevers? Puking? Rashes? Night sweats? The Big Guy thrashing in his candy cane bed?) But there was no need to panic. He'd been sick a long time. But it was probably just a bug. No one was allowed in to see him. And no one knew what the bug was, if it even was a bug, but it was probably a bug, something exotic he'd picked up in the vortex. And Ma Claus knew what to do about bugs. She was a fine doctor. Hadn't she kept both herself and the Big Guy in health for as long as anyone could remember? He just needed time and rest.

The bug story made sense. Despite the weirdness of vortex time, he was surely exposed to any number of nasty things every year, crossing time zones as he did, eating everyone's cookies, drinking everyone's milk. He'd been sick before, but he had a strong constitution; he'd always gotten better. For the time being, the Big Guy would be leaving all the planning and supervision to his capable elves. They knew what to do.

But could they do it? No one knew precisely how many elves they'd lost since last Christmas. And although Geimle didn't like to admit it, all the retooling he'd done for his special project had taken more time and more resources than he'd allowed for. He'd invested heavily in that one big sack of toys. It was hardly enough stock to serve a single American town, but it had used up the resources for half a continent. All this was revealed in the quarterly report of projected needs and available resources. Until then nobody knew, not even Geimle, how bad it really was. When Motto, Botto, and Gullnle returned, the boss just told them to get back to work as fast as possible, to work as hard as possible, and as for consequences of their little excursion, they'd sort things out after Christmas. Motto and Botto decided that was permission to return to the mailroom.

"Hey, it's not a parade, but it gets us off the planer," said Motto.

"We need a parade," said Botto.

Gullnle went back to package design and Karble to the office marked "Intrapole Communications Center." She'd made the sign herself.

Gully knocked on the door. "How did Geimle not figure out that you don't have an actual job?" There seemed to be a touch of jealousy in her voice.

35

A WEEK AFTER SHE LEFT, Claire was still sending occasional, vague texts, "Making progress." "Stay out of trouble." Things like that. When they tried to call, she never picked up.

When Morris asked his dad about her, he would just look up and smile and say, "She's fine. Don't worry. The girls can live without their mother for a few days."

"Have you talked to her?" Morris asked. But instead of "yes," or "no," he said, "I didn't think you two were getting along. And how are you doing with Tanya and Jasmine?" But he wouldn't wait for the answer. He'd just pat Morris on the head and tell him again that there was nothing to worry about and that he had a lot of work to do. And that was true. In fact, he wasn't home for much more than sleeping these days, but that was nothing out of the ordinary.

As for figuring out what Claire was up to, all they could do was look for clues and make guesses.

The first odd thing—they couldn't tell if it was a clue exactly— was that Claire seemed to have taken the elves' snow globe with her. Jasmine walked Tanya into the bedroom and showed her the place on her dresser where she'd seen it before their mother left. "She left her credit card, but she took that." The credit card was sitting on her dresser.

"It's probably just in her office," said Tanya.

"Why would she do that? She took them together and put them here together and then why would she lock the snow globe in her office and leave the credit card?"

"Maybe she thought we were gonna steal it?"

"We *gave* it to her."

Yeah, that didn't make sense. Besides, if she was worried about stealing, she wouldn't have left her credit card where anyone could pick it up. But just to be sure, they went out back and looked through the office window.

"She didn't even like it, but she seemed awfully attached to it," said Jasmine. And it was very inconvenient for travel, kind of large and bulky, hard to stuff into a suitcase—not the sort of thing you took to a business meeting.

The girls searched the bedroom without knowing what they were looking for. Nothing else even seemed remotely like a clue until Tanya picked up her mother's twenty-year-old, high school yearbook from the table beside her bed. Claire was not sentimental. And even if she were, who kept their old yearbook beside the bed? Most people kept things like that in boxes or put them on shelves with the things you never use but don't want to throw away. But here it was like a book to bore you into sleep on a bad night. She must have dug it up for some reason. And it did not take long for the girls to figure out what that was.

Willard Tremont. He was a goofy looking eighteen-year old in those days with big glasses, too much hair, and a ridiculous mustache. But there he was. And not only in his senior picture but in casual shots and pictures of school clubs—The Poetry Club and the Yearbook Club. And in a couple of those pictures, Claire was with him. Never beside him. The pictures didn't make the kids think he'd been a boyfriend or anything. But she knew him. And maybe he *had* been her boyfriend at some point. But that didn't really matter, did it? Even if he hadn't been that then, he still could be her boyfriend now. Sometimes people hook up with old friends from high school. She'd said she'd just met him on line. So apparently she hadn't told the truth about that. Certainly if she was going to lie about him, then he must be the one that was the problem, not that Mark Tortare.

Morris helped. Sitting on their parents' bed with a laptop, a smart phone, and a tablet, they searched the internet for any scrap they could. They found Willard Tremont's Facebook page. But it was set to maximum privacy, didn't even list his friends. He was listed as a friend on Claire's Facebook page but that yielded only his profile picture. He looked just as goofy now as he did then, but that information still wasn't helpful. He did not seem to have an account on Twitter or Tumblr or Instagram or any other site they could think of. It was a very rare name—only twenty-three of them in the whole United States according to a U.S. census site—so you'd think if he was anywhere on the internet, he'd be easy to find. But this just wasn't someone who spent a lot of time on social media. They managed to find an address. But the phone number didn't work.

Tanya huffed. She texted her mother. She got no response.

The doorbell rang. They all looked at each other. The doorbell sound was so rare in this house that Jasmine and Tanya had never heard it before.

"It's either a package or a preacher," said Morris.

"Or a pizza," said Tanya, hopefully.

But no one had ordered pizza, and as no one was interested in either of the other possibilities, Morris suggested they ignore it. But Jasmine went down the hall anyway. She came back with an envelope addressed to Claire. And it was from California.

"She would not want us to open that," said Tanya. Jasmine turned it over and over. It didn't give much away. It had a tab that you were supposed to pull to open it. There'd be no way to reseal it if you pulled that tab. Morris suggested they open it from the bottom. But it was very clear they couldn't do that either without mangling the envelope.

Jasmine's phone made a noise. It was a sound it had never made before, the sound of a bell. A picture of a vibrating bell appeared on the screen. She touched it.

Gully's face emerged. "Hey, how's it going?"

"What? How did you...?"

"Karble put this app on the phone. Cool, isn't it?" Jasmine couldn't figure out when Karble could have done that. But then, she *was* an elf after all. No wonder Santa Claus picked them for his delivery team. "Listen," said Gullnle, "don't tell Karble I'm using it."

"How could we do that?"

"You know, in case she calls. Give me the update."

Jasmine told her. She ended with, "We got this envelope." She held it up to the phone.

"Well open it," said Gully.

"She'll be mad," said Tanya.

"So?" said Gully.

Tanya grabbed it and pulled the tab. Jasmine gasped.

"If we open the bottom, she'll know we knew we were sneaking. If we pull the tab, we didn't know we were doing anything wrong."

No one really thought Claire was going to buy that, but the envelope was open. Inside was another envelope marked EAST LOS ANGELES DOCTORS HOSPITAL. It looked very old. There was no other writing on the envelope, and it wasn't sealed. It held a birth certificate. Someone named Tiara Williams.

Who was Tiara Williams?

There was nothing else in the envelope. And—they checked—there was no Tiara Williams in Claire's yearbook.

"I think you need to go to California," said Gully.

"How are we supposed to do that?" said Tanya.

"I'm not sure she knows we're not elves," said Morris.

36

THE CHILDREN DECIDED TO PLAY ignorant about the birth certificate, pretend it never came. The girls hid the envelope in their room.

Claire finally called. She said finding an agent was taking a little longer than expected. But everything was going okay. She sounded—happy. That was worrisome. She didn't usually sound happy. Home soon, she said. It had been almost two weeks.

"She must be on the fence," said Morris.

"Well then we'd better pull her off," said Jasmine.

"Or maybe she's already made up her mind. Maybe she's just trying to make us *think* she might come back."

"Why would she do that?" Tanya asked.

"We should find out," said Jasmine. Waiting was hard.

They all agreed, if she stayed away much longer it was because she preferred California and this Willard Tremont in Buena Vista to them and Indiana. Why Morris' dad wasn't more worried, they couldn't tell. Jasmine and Tanya wished they could go to California like Gully said.

A bell sounded on Morris' phone. It was Motto.

"Did they put that app on all our phones?"

Motto looked nervous. "Gully told us what she said. Not a good idea."

"Well it's not like we have a stable of reindeer in the backyard," said Morris.

"Look," said Motto, "have you tried talking to this Willard?"

"Have you got his phone number?" Jasmine asked.

Motto said they didn't do a lot of phone calling from the North Pole, not even to kids. And Willard Tremont didn't have any kids any more.

Karble's head showed up over Motto's shoulder on the screen: "Don't go to California."

"Do you guys have any idea how far California is from Indiana?" said Morris.

Motto got Karble up to date on the conversation.

"Oh," she said. "Well, doesn't your mother talk to him on her computer?"

"Her office is locked. It's always locked."

"Yeah, but didn't you say she left her credit card?" Karble asked.

Motto put his hand over the camera. "You can't tell them how to break into the room."

"We can still hear you," said Morris.

But apparently Motto didn't hear Morris.

Karble pushed Motto's hand away from the camera and pulled a stray strand of falling hair back over her ear. "I know how Malveno got in."

"Karble!"

Willard Tremont answered his Skype call as quickly as if he'd been waiting for it. His awkward face panned the computer screen as though he was trying to see his own reflection. He put a lit cigarette in his mouth. He still had a goofy mustache.

"We want to talk to Claire," said Tanya.

"I thought you were Claire," he said.

"Isn't she with you?" said Jasmine.

Willard showed them the whole room with his webcam (which was somewhere between artsy messy and just plain messy) then set it back in front of his face. He peered over his glasses, his hands shook faintly. Smoke rose from a cigarette. His eyes shifted from face to face. A smile decided it was okay to come out. "Let me see," he said, "Tanya," he pointed, "Mo Li…"

"Huh," said Jasmine.

"Mo Li," he said again. "Jasmine."

"What?" Jasmine's jaw dropped.

"Lost most of my Mandarin," he said, "but I'm pretty sure about that. And… and you'd be Morris, the stepson."

He looked nervous but also like someone who always looked nervous. But he wasn't afraid to talk.

"So she *was* there?" said Morris.

"A week or two ago. We talked about her book."

"She came all the way to California just to talk about a book?"

"Does that seem odd to you? A lot of agents in California. And now she's getting back into writing."

"She never stopped writing," said Tanya.

"Books," said Willard, "stories. Blogs and magazines are not the same thing. She's picking up where she left off. It doesn't surprise me at all that she came here to talk about it. I know some people. I would have thought she was back home by now."

"She never came home."

"Well, let's call her. Don't know why you didn't do that in the first place." He reached for his phone.

"No," Tanya and Jasmine yelled together.

He cast a look of suspicion. "Why not?"

They looked at each other. And as no one could come up with anything half as plausible as the truth, they told him that.

To their surprise, he didn't find their story at all crazy. In fact, given the half-finished condition of the manuscript she'd sent him, he said he wouldn't be surprised if the trip to see him wasn't designed as an alibi, a cover story. Something more important might just be going on. But he had no idea what it was. He wasn't the kind of person to give false comfort. He did nothing to discredit their idea that she might be in the process of abandoning them.

"Could you answer some questions for us?" asked Jasmine.

He said he was happy to. He answered every one of their questions and even offered information they had not thought to look for. He'd known Claire for twenty-five years. They'd stayed in touch.

"Why didn't she ever mention you before?"

"Do you tell her about all your friends?" he asked.

"Yeah, but why did she tell us she met you in a chat room?"

"Well, she did," he said. They reconnected pretty recently on Facebook—which he was not fond of. And she'd got him into this online writer's group where they talked about books and publishing. He and Claire had been friends throughout high school. They shared an interest in writing. They worked on yearbooks together, the literary magazine, the newspaper. They took a lot of the same English classes. They couldn't avoid daily contact. Had he ever been her boyfriend? That made him laugh, a low, two-note, nervous laugh. If he'd just denied it, they might have thought he was lying, but the spontaneous laugh was hard to misread. And anyway, he seemed almost unnaturally honest—the kind of person you'd better not tell a secret to.

"I would've been," he said. "But I'm pretty she wouldn't't've. And she was never between boyfriends long enough for me to ask." They were friends, that's all. But even if they hadn't been, everyone knew Claire's story. She was just one of those kids who did things that everyone talked about. "She told everyone she was going to be a writer. It was all she wanted to do. When we were all getting set to go to college, she said there was no need. They only care about what you write. I tried to tell her that was a mistake. And then of course, when she got pregnant, that kind of put an end to that."

"What?" Tanya said. "She... but I'm not that old."

He let out another nervous laugh: "She never told you? Well maybe I shouldn't've." It was the first time he'd sounded reluctant. "I should probably go."

"No, you should tell us," said Jasmine. "You already started, so it's worse if you don't. Did she give it up? Did she have an abortion?"

"Maybe she's trying to find her lost daughter," said Tanya. "We have a sister. Maybe it's this..."

"She died." Willard put out his cigarette. All the air drained from the room. "It was a car accident. If I remember right, they went around the corner too fast. The car skidded off the road. The car seat failed. Sorry to be the one to tell you."

"Really?" Jasmine looked baffled.

"People die in car accidents all the time," said Willard.

"Was that the same one that killed her parents?"

Willard looked at Jasmine. "Whose parents?"

"Mom's. They died in a car crash. Was it the same one?"

Willard sucked his lips into his mouth so that his mustache seemed to be connected directly to his chin. "You have to take that up with Claire." He picked up his pack of cigarettes, looked at it, and put it down.

"You're not going to tell us?"

"It's not my place," he said.

"Okay, okay," said Jasmine. "Who is Tiara Williams?"

He looked shocked. "I'm sorry," he said. And the connection went dead.

"He changed his tune pretty fast." Morris said.

"How did he know my Chinese name?"

"What difference does that make?" Tanya asked.

"Mom doesn't even know my Chinese name."

"She'd have to," said Morris. "It would be on a piece of paper."

"She never told me. She never looked it up. And Willard said he just got back in touch with her after twenty-five years, but he knew my name. He's hiding something."

"Yeah, that is weird," said Tanya.

"How do we know she wasn't in that house the whole time?" said Jasmine. "He only showed us that one room."

"And another thing," said Jasmine, "how come everyone's dying in car crashes?"

Tanya's and Jasmine's phones pinged simultaneously. A text from Claire: DONE. Be home tonight.

"Do you think he told her?"

"We can't trust him," said Morris.

37

CLAIRE WAS UNUSUALLY QUIET when she returned from California. It was as though California had slapped her across the face. She wasn't angry or happy. She was calm—and cool. She hugged her daughters without conviction. She reached a hand out to them when she passed by them in the hallway or the kitchen. She touched them on the arm or on the back. But she did it the way someone might touch a piece of furniture to remind herself it was there and it was hers. She stayed that way for weeks. She never asked about the envelope, as though she hadn't known it was coming.

When they asked her about California, she said, "Looks like I might have a publisher for my book." But they knew from Willard that the book wasn't ready to even show to a publisher.

The children were dying to know who Tiara Williams was. But they couldn't figure out how to ask. The elves tried to help. But they only deepened the confusion. Karble told her that there was a Tiara Williams to whom they'd delivered toys for four years starting the year of the birth certificate. And then she was gone from their records. But then, it wasn't such an unusual name. This might not be the one.

"Or maybe she died," said Tanya.

Tanya of course first thought of the dead sister that Willard had told them about. But that sister died as a baby, and this Tiara was much too old to have been her.

It was all very worrisome.

They wanted to ask Willard more questions. But they were sure he'd already told Claire about their first conversation. That left them with nothing to do but to look into Mark Tortare. He was all over the internet, very easy to find, but he ignored every attempt to contact him. As he was a lawyer, they even made up a story as though they were possible clients and contacted him at his law office. That didn't work either. So they gave up on him too—if he really was interested in Claire he'd have said something back, right?—and they brought their attention back on Willard.

Jasmine asked Claire what happened to the snow globe. She said, "Why you so concerned with that toy?"

Nothing was working. And there was nothing more they could do. They had to just wait it out. Maybe nothing was going to happen. It no longer seemed like Claire was trying to run away. So what did it matter? Maybe she had gone to California to see Willard but ended up breaking up with him. They knew better than to trust anything Willard had said. Sure, he'd *seemed* honest on Skype, but everyone in California is some kind of actor. And things had gotten back to almost normal. Claire spent the days in her basement office. Morris' dad spent his days at work. Jasmine played her guitar. Morris played video games. Tanya hung out with her friends and brought them to the house. Every once in a while, for a break and to get him away from the video games, Jasmine talked Morris into bike trips, which got longer and longer.

It was the elves more than the children who kept the question of what Claire was up to open, calling one or another of them, checking in at random intervals to see how the "investigation" was going.

Gully could not accept the lack of news: "We've got a strange birth certificate, an unexplained trip to California, and a missing, deluxe snow globe. *That* is a mystery." She said this to the kids over the phone and again to Karble at the North Pole. Both the kids and Karble said the same thing in reply.

"It's probably for her book." When the kids said this, Gully just nodded and ended the conversation. When Karble said it, she replied, "Who orders a birth certificate for a book? I don't know how humans do things, but I doubt they'd even send you a birth certificate for a book."

Karble had to admit that was probably true. It would have to be some birth certificate you had a right to—like a family member's.

Gully updated Motto and Botto. Botto thought it was just an error in the human bookkeeping system. Motto thought maybe Claire was just trying to make sure she had the name spelled right. "Humans have a thing about spelling," he said. Gully said there was only one way to make sense of all the facts, and it was this: Claire was really a private investigator engaged by this Mark Tortare to investigate the cold-case death of his cousin, Tiara Williams. Motto thought that was brilliant. Botto saw no holes in it. Gully wanted to tell the children they'd figured it out.

Karble wasn't so sure.

"Don't you think we need some actual evidence first?"

"No," said Gully. "But if you insist, let's just grab Donder and Blitzen and shoot on down to California and get some. That could be fun."

"What about wrapping paper?" said Karble.

"Oh, yeah."

"Besides, Haymin's guarding the barn like it's the last stash of mistletoe before the apocalypse," said Botto.

But Gully thought getting past Haymin's guards would just add to the fun.

They decided to keep thinking about it—which was something that the schedule, as it turned out, left them almost no time to do. Production always geared up this time of year, late summer in the Northern Hemisphere, but it was worse this time around: as always, they had all the free daylight they could possibly want and billions of toys to produce, but now they had fewer elves to produce them with and no Big Guy to supervise the supervisors or manage the managers. Geimle and the other managers had everyone working flat out. Motto suspected that another reason for the busyness was to keep the workforce from thinking about the absence of the Big Guy. Was he *still* sick? No one had seen him since Christmas. And the rumors Gully had mentioned expanded like frost—though the wiser elves understood they were absurd. One said that he wasn't even in the castle, that he'd taken a sled into the wide world somewhere and, disguised as a regular old man, had been undergoing treatment for some unknown and possibly fatal malady. Another, even harder to believe, said that he had quietly retired to Burzee himself along with all the fleeing elves, that they were transitioning to a Santa-less operation, a post-Santa era at Claus, Ltd. although they'd continue to use his head and image, as though he was the dead C.E.O. of an American fast food company.

And no one thought *that* would work. If the Big Guy was really gone, Motto gave it three years before pressures from the melting ice cap and tensions among the elves caused them to abandon the whole operation.

"I wonder if the humans would even notice?" said Botto.

"Isn't that where we started?" said Gullnle.

"They'd probably just pretend we're still here, pass around gifts in our name, just like they kind of do already, really."

"It wouldn't be the same," said Karble, but she couldn't say exactly how. She was very carefully trimming a Burzee rose at the time.

"It would be like if you took the horn section out of a symphony," said Motto. "Even if you gave what you could to the strings, it would make the whole performance disappointing."

"I just can't get over how bad Geimle would look in the big red suit," said Gully.

"On the other hand," said Botto, "I think I would be perfect for the job."

38

TANYA FOUND THE NOTE ON THE TABLE on the first day of school: "Gone to California. Be good."

Tanya showed the note to Jasmine and Morris.

Jasmine stared at the paper like she didn't know what it was.

"So she waited until school started," said Morris.

Jasmine ran to Claire's bedroom. She wanted to see what was missing. She was expecting to find it cleared out. But nothing appeared to be missing. The closet was full of clothes. So were the dressers. "So she's coming back," said Jasmine.

"She could just buy new stuff," said Morris. "There's nothing here she couldn't live without."

"She doesn't do that," said Tanya. "She doesn't buy stuff she already has."

"Maybe she's got a really rich guy. That lawyer, he's rich. Or maybe she's going to change her whole identity."

Jasmine and Tanya looked at each other. Their mother was very careful with money. But they couldn't absolutely deny the possibility.

"Okay," said Jasmine. "What *did* she have that she couldn't live without?"

They ran down to her office.

It was unlocked—which made them hesitant to go in. But not for long. Tanya pushed the door open. The books were all there, so was the printer. There were three pens on the desk and a pad of legal paper turned to a page with writing all over it. The coffee cup still had coffee in it. Her desk was cluttered as always. But in the middle was clean and empty space where her computer had been.

"It *is* a laptop," said Jasmine.

There was no way to know what else might be missing.

Jasmine called her mother—no answer. She left a voice mail. Tanya sent her a text. No response there either.

"She could be busy," said Tanya. "Or her phone could be off."

"She's gone," said Jasmine.

"She wouldn't just go," said Tanya. "She wouldn't *leave* us. She wouldn't."

"But she did," said Morris. The girls looked at each other. Jasmine fell into the chair and Tanya plunked herself down on the desk. They didn't say anything. Morris left the room. He didn't want to be the one to tell his dad. So he called the North Pole. Gullnle answered.

"I'll get right back to you," she said.

Minutes later, Jasmine got a text. It was from Botto: "Don't do anything."

"Don't *do* anything?" Like there was something they could have done? Like you're floating on a sheet of ice in the middle of the ocean and someone yells, "just stay there." Jasmine showed the text to Tanya. Meanwhile Claire too had sent a text: "Sorry to run off like that."

Of course they asked for an explanation. But they didn't get it. "Talk to you soon," she said.

Jasmine said, "What does that mean?"

Tanya texted, "Are you coming home?"

Claire responded, "Sorry, gotta go. Be good."

Then she texted, "Not now." Then she stopped texting.

"What does that mean?" said Morris.

"I means she's either going to come back and get us or she isn't," said Tanya.

It was a Tuesday. Morris' dad always stayed out late on Tuesdays. He went out to eat after work with his buddies and then they played cards or video games. Morris finally called him and told him about the note. "Yes, of course. Quite a shame."

"What's going on?" said Morris.

"I'm sure Claire will tell you when she's ready." And then he paused. "There's frozen pizza in the fridge. Get to bed on time."

Morris made the pizza, but he was the only one who ate any.

He was alone in the kitchen the next day with the rest of the pizza when a knock came on the door—the back door, the sliding glass door. He yelled to his stepsisters.

Botto and Gullnle had their faces pressed against the glass. They beckoned to the kids and pointed to the reindeer that were foraging in the backyard.

"You cannot imagine how hard it was to steal a reindeer anymore," said Gullnle. "Grab that pizza. It's a long way to Minnesota."

"Minnesota?" said Morris.

"And bring your winter coats, and hats, and gloves, and boots," said Botto.

"Oh—" said Gullnle. "And bring me that birth certificate."

The children all looked confused, but Tanya ran to her room to get it.

"Perfect," said Gullnle noticing the unsealed, blank envelope. "Give me a pen." She wrote the kids' address in fine elven calligraphy on the envelope and asked for a stamp. "We're going to take it with us and mail it back from California. And then when Claire gets it, you're going to ask her who this Tiara Williams is. I'm dying to know."

It was decided that Morris should stay behind so his dad didn't get suspicious. A handful of excuses if his father happened to ask about the whereabouts of the girls would suffice.

The vortex door was now in Minnesota. So this was going to take a little while. The elves had another key. Geimle had confiscated the duplicate key Botto had made, but he hadn't confiscated the marzipan replica. So Botto had made a third key. Motto duplicated the harp from memory and showed Gullnle exactly how to play it. He'd played it so many times, he knew the tuning and every quality of the sound. And as for the blue flame, it turned out that was just flame. Any oversized flame would do.

Once the reindeer were air bound, they flew pretty fast. But it still took several hours in the shivering cold. The girls sat behind the elves. And although the backsides of the deer had ample room, and their legs were tied to a leather blanket that wasn't really a saddle so they couldn't fall off (Motto had insisted on this and Karble had fashioned it before they left the pole; elves never used such things), the long ride in that position made their thighs ache and their butts tingle.

Cold and hungry and achy, the girls found themselves in the early evening in rural Minnesota. The vortex door was in a cornfield through which they had to weave carefully. There didn't seem to be much fear that people would notice them, but they didn't want to flatten whole rows of corn. People might think the farm had been visited by aliens. It became clearer every time they met that elves don't try very hard not to be noticed, but people for the most part failed to notice them. When Tanya asked about this, Gullnle said it was because of a kind of magical aura elves give off. Botto however had never heard of such a thing. And although Gullnle insisted it was true, Botto thought it was just that most people weren't very good at noticing things.

Inside the vortex, they grabbed about half a bushel of corn for the deer and then headed for a diner Botto had spotted from the air: Freddie's Family Restaurant. Gully set the table while Botto went into the kitchen to get some food.

"One hand on the plate at all times," he said putting a burger and fries in front of each of the girls.

"We've been very good to Freddie's family over the years. I only wish he knew how he was helping us out now," said Gully.

It was odd to be sitting down in a diner peopled with stone-still patrons in funny poses awkwardly paused in the eating of their dinners. In the booth behind them, an older couple were clearly in animated conversation. The man was pointing at the woman sternly with a ketchup-covered French fry. Her face looked back in disbelief. Between them and the counter five tables had been pushed together to accommodate a young soccer team who did not appear to have won the game they were celebrating.

"Is everybody always unhappy about something?" asked Jasmine.

"Sure," said Gully. "If they dig deep enough. If you don't have an unhappiness right there on the surface, you can always find one somewhere underneath if you need it."

Tanya didn't like the sound of that. "Yeah, but happy works the same way."

"I don't know," said Botto. "Mostly, sure, perhaps. There are some people with nothing much to be happy about. They can dig all the way to the bottom. But there isn't anyone with nothing to be sad about."

"I don't agree," said Gully.

"They're alive, aren't they," said Jasmine. "That's something to be happy about."

"But what's so happy about that if you've got nothing else?"

"Because if you're alive, things could always change," said Gullnle. "In fact, things *will* always change, because that's what things do. That's what being alive means."

"Except in the vortex," said Botto.

"Even in the vortex," said Gullnle. "Just here they aren't in a hurry about it."

It was awkward having to hold on to the plates and the forks while eating.

The girls wanted to eat fast and get going.

Gully reminded them that there is no rush once you're in the vortex. And the girls understood that. But they were still anxious to get to California.

"Rest your bottom," said Botto. "We'll be back on Comet and Flossie soon enough."

"And get good and warm," said Gully. "You think you were cold last time. It's even colder in the vortex."

That was not a surprise. Just as everything was grayer inside, everything was always a little cooler too, like stepping into an air-conditioned warehouse. The girls had felt it as soon as they went through the door.

When they left Freddie's Family Diner, Gullnle hopped on Flossie with Jasmine and headed south. Botto yelled for her to turn around, but she kept going until Jasmine tapped her on the shoulder.

"What? Oh? I wonder what he wants." She flew back. By this point Botto and Tanya had mounted Comet.

"California is that way," he said.

"Oops."

"It's not that hard," said Botto. "Toward the sunset."

Setting, however, was just what the sun was not doing. In fact it rose. If you could stare at it, and you almost could, you would be able to see it rise as they covered the ground toward California, the only moving thing in the vortex other than themselves. Botto had researched some more good places to eat, and Gullnle remembered the map Karble had given them. They stopped to sleep only once, and that they did only for the sake of the tired humans. The sun stopped moving then. It was late afternoon when they landed the deer in front of Willard Tremont's house.

Willard himself with his goofy mustache was sitting on a recliner. He was dressed in a somewhat tightfitting dark suit and navy tie, and although his plump body and bedraggled hair made it impossible for him to bring off the neatness implied by the suit and tie, the very attempt contrasted with the clutter of his surroundings. Now that they were here they could see there was no pretense at all toward "artsy." Books were everywhere on the floor in piles that were high enough beside all the seating places to serve as wobbly end tables. Some even had ashtrays on them full of cigarette butts. Tanya and Jasmine could not remember having seen ashtrays before, though they'd heard of them and they'd known people who smoked. And there were piles of newspapers, which also seemed to put the room back decades. Perhaps he didn't spend as much time on the computer as they thought. But he was on the computer right now; it was on his lap. A cloud of smoke encircled his head.

"Outside the vortex it would smell even worse," said Botto.

"Why's he dressed like that," said Tanya.

"What difference does that make?" said Gullnle.

"I don't know. It just seems funny a guy that lives like this wears a suit."

"We need to look for mom," said Jasmine.

Tanya wrinkled her face. "Do you really think she'd leave us for this?"

"He might be a perfectly nice guy. You can't tell," said Gully.

"All this crap everywhere, and smoking. She might not be the neatest person in the world, but this is impossible. If she wanted this guy, she'd have to bring us just to do the chores around here."

Jasmine had to agree with that. Though her office might be cluttered, Claire made sure someone cleaned up the kitchen before bed and put things back where they belonged.

But still, she might have been here. Having come all the way here, they looked for signs.

It was a split level house. There were not a lot of rooms. They found a printout picture of Claire, Tanya and Jasmine on his dresser, a picture the girls were familiar with; it was on their mother's Facebook page. It was odd, because there were no other photographs lying about in the house. So clearly Claire was someone special to him.

"And notice that you *are* both in the picture," said Gullnle. "That's a good sign."

But there was no sign that Claire had ever been there in person.

They sat down on the couch and two chairs in the living room to figure out what was next. Botto brought them what food he could find from the fridge. "Elves' privilege," he said when Jasmine seemed to look at him funny. "He got plenty of gifts as a kid."

"But you said…" said Jasmine.

"Elves' privilege," he repeated.

"She's not here and she hasn't been here," said Tanya. "Did we bring the address of the other guy?"

"Mark something," said Jasmine.

They'd been so fixated on Willard Tremont, they couldn't remember the other guy's name.

"Turtle? Tercher? Torture?" said Tanya.

Jasmine looked back at Willard as though looking there would somehow jog her memory. Gullnle followed her gaze.

"He's got a phone book," said Gully.

"Who has phone books anymore," said Botto. "He's sure having a hard time getting out of the twentieth century."

"So if we can remember the name, we can look up the address."

Jasmine walked over to the man. Willard was staring intently at his computer screen. He had a folded newspaper in his lap. He also had something in the chair with him between his hip and the arm, something almost hidden. It was made of glass. She reached down to get it. It was wedged in there, and even though she knew he was in a kind of suspended animation, she still felt weird getting that close, as though she were reaching out to touch a dead guy, or as though she might wake him.

"What is it?" said Tanya.

"I think it's…." and then she hauled it out. "She *was* here."

Jasmine held Claire's Christmas snow globe in front on her. They all went over to look at it.

"She must have left it here."

"She might have given it to him as a present."

"No, she liked it too much. She was just showing it to him," said Jasmine. "We should bring it back to her."

"And how would you explain that?" said Gullnle.

"She probably doesn't even know she left it. We'll just sneak it in her suitcase."

"Won't it just disappear as soon as we let go of it?" said Tanya.

"I don't know," said Botto. "We brought it into the vortex. Then Claire touched it outside the vortex. I have no idea."

Jasmine put it on the counter and let go of it. It stayed there.

"So everything ever brought in at Christmas is different from everything that wasn't?" Botto wondered.

"Wow," said Gullnle. "I didn't know that."

"Oh, and that's saying something!" said Botto. "She never admits that."

"He was at a funeral," said Tanya. She didn't find the logic of the vortex or Gullnle's quirks all that interesting. Willard's computer screen was open to Facebook, which told her nothing. But the newspaper in his hand was folded to the obituary page. The name "Williams," had caught her eye. "Isn't that the name on the birth certificate?"

Gullnle took it out.

"Did Tiara Williams die?" said Jasmine.

"No. James Williams. He died. His funeral was today." She looked at the kitchen clock. "It was three hours ago in Yorba Linda."

"That's a pretty common name," said Botto. "We get hundreds of letters from Williamses every year."

"What if Tiara became James—and then died?" said Gullnle.

"No, not that," said Tanya. "The paper says he is survived by his son Mark Tortare of Yorba Linda, his daughter Tiara and four grandchildren."

"So that's him," said Jasmine.

"It must be," said Tanya.

Gullnle grabbed the paper. "Why doesn't Tiara have a family name?"

"Probably because it's Williams," said Tanya. "But really, why would someone send this woman's birth certificate to our house?"

"I thought she died when she was four," said Gullnle.

39

NOW THAT THEY HAD THE NAME, the address wasn't hard to find. Willard Tremont's phone book didn't cover Yorba Linda. But some people did still have phone books in Yorba Linda too. When Botto announced the address, Gullnle announced that it was in "the pricey part of town." But from the vantage of Comet and Flossie high above the ground, that description didn't seem to narrow things down very much. Yorba Linda appeared to be made almost entirely of pricey homes squished uncomfortably close together. Mark Torare's house was a big, brown, brick-front building with a three-car garage door. There was a van in the driveway and three palm trees in the yard. Further back were the hills.

Upon seeing the place, the girls wondered aloud why they'd ever thought their mother was interested in Willard Tremont and not Mark Tortare.

The front door was locked, but the garage was not. It opened to a large, empty space, a place you could play in on a rainy day if it ever rained in Yorba Linda.

There were half-full trays of food on the kitchen counter and there were baskets of flowers all over the living room, which is where they found Claire. She was sitting half sideways on the couch with a little girl cuddled up beside her. And she was smiling. On the floor was another girl distracted by a video game that was just slightly out of phase on her screen. Behind the couch was the man himself—Mark Tortare—slim and dignified; he had a small plate of half-eaten food in each hand. He appeared to be cleaning up the room after the guests had left. He looked like a lawyer would want to look in front of a judge or a jury, tall with just a little grey in his hair. He was crisply dressed in a pressed black suit. He hadn't even loosened his tie. One hand was raised higher than the other as though he was explaining something. Everyone was dressed in black. Claire was wearing a dress the girls had never seen before and a little black hat. That they had come from a funeral was obvious from the clothes but not from the expressions on their faces. Claire was smiling unusually bright, and the girl beside her was giggling, and the girl on the floor was lost in her game. The event did not seem to have left anyone sad. The picture seemed so much more domestic than anything Jasmine or Tanya could remember from their own lives.

"What if she doesn't bring us?" said Jasmine.

"Oh," said Gullnle. "She wouldn't do that. I'm sure of it."

"Based on what?" said Botto.

Gully gave him a quick elbow to the stomach, "I'm just sure."

"Why would she want us when she's happy?" said Tanya.

"She came all the way here for a funeral? She rushed here to go to a funeral for some guy she never met. What does that tell you?" said Jasmine.

"It tells you that she wants to comfort this guy that just lost his dad."

"You don't do that for someone you just met on Facebook," said Jasmine. "And you don't do it for a guy who wants to see you get your book published. You do it for family."

"So she already feels like she's part of this guy's family," said Tanya.

"It is a nice house," said Botto.

"We wouldn't fit here," said Tanya. "Look how neat it is."

"Lord & Taylor, military neat," said Jasmine. They'd stayed with a guy like that once, every toothpick where it belonged. It was awful.

"What are you saying?" said Gullnle.

"Just if she takes us with her, it could be hell for us and hell for her and she'd leave this guy in a month and then where would we be? Willard Tremont's spare bedroom? And she knows that. If she wants this life, she doesn't want us to be part of it."

"Don't say that," said Botto.

"You don't know that," said Gullnle.

Tanya looked like she was going to cry—for just a second. She didn't let herself. No, she stomped around the room and pulled books from shelves and pillows from couches and tossed them all over the place just pushing them over her shoulders without even turning around to see where they went.

"What are you doing?" yelled Jasmine.

"Making it look like actual people live here." She didn't turn around.

"But..." said Jasmine.

The elves poked each other.

"They just go back," said Jasmine. And Tanya turned around to see the neatness untouched. Every book was back on the shelf, arranged by height. The elves were trying not to laugh, but Tanya didn't find it funny at all. She groaned, a long deep groan, from the bottom of her stomach to her nose. "I can't do anything."

"You can't *change* anything," said Botto.

Tanya ran over to her mother. She balled her fists up and shook them.

Jasmine ran over to her. "What are you gonna do?"

"I want to do something," she said.

"Wait," said Gullnle. And she ran outside to where the reindeer were chewing on Mark Tortare's perfect grass. In a moment she came back with Geimle's snow globe in her hands. She put it in Claire's lap.

"You can't do that," said Botto.

"What good is that going to do?" Jasmine asked.

"No idea," said Gullnle. "But it is something, right. Tanya's right. Sometimes you've just got to do *something*."

"But there are rules," said Botto. "You can't make it look like magic."

"You haven't followed a rule since Christmas," said Gullnle. Botto picked up the toy and placed it on the floor by Claire's foot beside her purse. "At least that much," he said. "We don't want her to freak."

Tanya sighed.

Jasmine picked up her mother's purse. Inside she found what she was looking for: a boarding pass. The plane would leave from San Francisco tomorrow morning. So this wasn't it. She hadn't yet abandoned them. She'd be home in the afternoon.

"Well, then," said Botto. We just have to convince her to stay in Indiana. How hard could that be?"

"How do we do that?" said Tanya.

"I don't see how she could live here anyway," said Jasmine. "She's not that much neater than any than the rest of us. She'd go crazy in a week having to wipe off her toothbrush before she put it back in the holder."

The question on the long flight home was whether they should reveal what they knew to Claire. It would be easy enough to prove that they knew what she was up to, but not at all easy to explain *how* they knew. And of course she would ask. She wouldn't believe the truth. And Botto and even Gullnle said they could not be part of the explanation. "We're in plenty of trouble as it is. We *really* can't be showing ourselves to Claire."

"Children are one thing," said Botto. "And anyway, *you* found *us*. That doesn't usually happen. We usually just walk around and no one notices."

"But if we start going up to people and saying, 'hi, I'm an elf. Let me show you the vortex,' that could lead to exile."

"Burzee, here we come!"

Jasmine could not see the logic in it, after all they'd done: stealing reindeer, sneaking away, taking kids into the vortex, running away from their supervisor.

"Just too risky," said Gullnle. "I like my job."

"But this is our mother," said Tanya.

"It would be one thing if there was a point to it," said Gullnle. "But it wouldn't solve the actual problem, would it? It would just be to show how you know there is a problem. You'd still have to solve the problem just as you have to now. All that risk and no payoff? No. Sorry."

40

EVERY CHAIR AT THE BIG OAK TABLE in Geimle's office was taken—every chair except, of course, the plush velvet one at the head. That had been empty all year. The managers' council hadn't heard so much as a word out of the Big Guy since Christmas. Geimle had as usual sent reports of every meeting up to the castle. And every time, as though in reply, Ma Claus sent news of the Big Guy's condition—always positive, always informing the team how sure she was the he was on the mend or about to turn the corner, always telling them not to worry. But there was never anything to indicate that anyone had read Geimle's reports. Not that the Big Guy had ever been a really hands-on administrator. Even when he was healthy—as he usually was—he had often avoided production meetings. He trusted the elves to do their work, and they always came through. But such a *long* silence was unnerving. The Big Guy literally did not know anything that was going on. He'd had the electronics office install all these monitors, presumably to keep track of operations, but there was no sign he'd ever used them. Certainly if he knew anything of the unusual events of the past year—the trickle of disappearing elves, or Motto and Botto and Gullnle and Karble's unauthorized use of reindeer, or even Geimle's own scheme to spread a special Summer Christmas into North America—surely he'd have said something. Geimle imagined all these monitors from all over the North Pole feeding a constant stream of words and pictures into the Big Guy's empty office in the North Wing. He must be alarmingly sick.

Now that everyone had taken a seat at the table, Haymin rose. The head of the reindeer barns looked carefully from face to face at all the managers. And then he announced to all that Comet and Flossie were gone—despite all his precautions.

Geimle shook his head and huffed.

Malveno snickered.

Haymin looked down disapprovingly. "Something is going on up here that we don't know about. I say it's time we tell the Big Guy directly. Someone has got to go up there. And when one of the managers asked him how he knew it wasn't just a couple of clever and prankish elves he said, "Because this is beyond clever. It's organized. No matter how much security I put on the barns, someone manages to get whatever they want whenever they want it." And then he directed everyone's attention to the screen at the front of the room. He pressed a button and started a recording of surveillance footage. "Notice this, this is footage from the time of the theft. The picture shows both deer in their stalls right here." He pointed to the time stamp in the corner. "Then it switches to the front door. This would have been the moment the deer were unhitched. The picture then moves to a long view of the south end of the barn—Flossie and Comet were side by side in the north. Now listen carefully. You can hear them walking across the floor. Now the picture switches to the east. This is the moment when the door is opening. You can just hear it slowly moving like the thieves know they've got all the time in the world. Then we move back to an inside shot of the east. This would be just after they get outside. Now on a normal scan, we should have gone back to the north before going to this next shot, which shows the outdoor view. I find that odd. But see here, in this exterior shot the door's already closed. But look at this—these are fresh tracks in the snow. Two elves. Two deer. By the time the frame hovers back to the west side of the north wing and we finally see that the deer are gone, the thieves have had plenty of time to get airborne."

"Could be just dumb luck," said Malveno.

"Could be two elves have taken the quick route to Burzee," said Philona.

"It was planned," said Haymin.

"Who's missing?" said Geimle.

Maynle, head of the mailroom, said Botto hadn't come in yesterday or today. Phoxin said she hadn't seen Gullnle in package design.

"Why would Botto and Gully head for Burzee?" said Maynle. "You didn't even demote them after their recent lark."

"We have to inform the Big Guy, pronto. If you can't control your elves..." said Haymin.

"How are we supposed to control elves?" said Geimle.

"You don't see any barn elves stealing reindeer, hightailing it to Burzee."

"They weren't actually stolen," said Malveno. "The deer will come back on their own eventually."

"I'm not holding back any more reports." Haymin took an envelope out of a bag and held it in front of him. "Someone is going to hand deliver this to the Big Guy and someone's going to tell him everything that's going on here when he does. We all know that's your job, Geimle. But if you won't do it, I will."

Geimle took the envelope. He promised he'd go to the castle as soon as the production meeting was over. It was past time. And he and the Big Guy had a lot to talk about.

To Geimle's surprise, the ornate door of Burzee oak at the castle entrance was not opened by Minina. It was opened by Karble.

"Karble?" he said. "Why are *you* in the castle?"

"Oh, just came to see if I could see the Big Guy. Not available. Too sick."

"About what?"

"Yeah, so what is up with Haymin? Not like him to lose reindeer. Thought I'd head up the barns and see if I can fix the rotation scheme on those cameras."

Well, that raised some questions. Geimle crossed the threshold. "Why would you drag your tools up here if you're going down to the barns?"

"Busy day, you know. Fewer elves, that's more work for everyone."

"Yes. That was the theme of our…" Geimle stopped. Karble was smiling too brightly. "Well, you get back to work. We'll talk later."

Geimle made a move toward the stairs.

"You can't go up there. Ma won't let anyone in. He's just too sick."

"Maybe I can talk through the door." Geimle headed toward the stairs. Karble bolted past him. "He… he… he's incoherent," she said. And she jumped up the stairs and stretched an arm toward each railing to block his way.

"I think if he'll talk to you, he'll talk to me."

"No, really, can't talk. Just lies there. He hates to be seen that way."

"Then I'll just have to talk to Ma."

And then another voice came down the stairs, "Geimle, haven't seen you in the castle in ages." For a moment he hoped it was Ma Claus, coming to unblock his way. But from around the corner came the white smile of Minina.

"Just coming to see the Big Guy, if I may. Or Ma, if I can't."

"Oh, he's too sick and she's too busy nursing him," said Minina, holding an expression that did not seem quite sincere. "But I'll be sure to take your envelope and tell them you stopped by."

Geimle hesitated. It wasn't clear—as was often the case when you got outside the factories—who outranked whom in this situation. He had never been Karble's direct manager, and he had no authority over Minina, who'd always worked in the castle. But as he could not detect any real concern in Minina's voice, he moved gently past Karble's blockade and continued up the stairs.

Karble grabbed his arm lightly as he passed. "Don't go up there."

He tapped her benignly on her head. "I've seen sick people before."

When Geimle reached the top of the stairs, Minina said, "He's asked me not to let anyone in. You can't see him." Geimle still thought he detected more urgency to stop him than concern for the Big Guy.

"You're worrying me, Minina."

"He was very firm," she said.

"Then I'll be sure to tell him it was my fault that I did not listen to you." Minina grabbed his arm as Karble had done, but she did not hold on as he turned down the hallway.

Karble and Minina were standing behind him when he reached the door. They did not try to block it.

"It would be better if you didn't," said Minina.

Karble said, "I'll tell him about Botto and Gully, and about Flossie and Comet and how far production is behind."

"What? How do you even know...?" Geimle tapped gently on the door.

"He already knows," she said, "he said he was sure you'd pull through the crisis. You always do."

There was no answer at the door. Geimle knocked louder and called out. "Hey, Big Guy. It's Geimle. I just need a word."

Still no answer. Just a lot of humming and clicking, like the sounds of machines on the other side. He thought of medical equipment and the Big Guy hooked to all those outrageous contraptions to keep him alive.

He eased open the door open. Karble took out her phone.

The big four-poster bed with the candy cane headboard and the quilted canopy and counterpane stood in the middle of the room as it always had, its ornate curtains pulled back as one would think would not be so if the man in the bed had been sick a long time and needed to stay warm. But the covers were neatly arranged and the pillows in their quilted cases were fluffed up full. And there was no one in the bed. And there was no one in the rocking chair beside the bed where Ma Claus or anyone nursing a sick man would have sat. There was no one in the room at all. No empty plates, no scraps of food, no medicine, no half-drunk glasses of water or cider or hot chocolate or coffee. No medical machines either. No sign at all that anyone had lain in that bed recently or that anyone sick had ever been here. The sound of the machines was the sound of surveillance. The wall behind Geimle was covered from the chair rail to the ceiling with monitors and speakers—flashing pictures that revealed every corner of the North Pole, all the factories, all the assembly rooms, all the meeting rooms, and Haymin's barns. And in front of the screens was a chair, a small, plush chair, a chair much too small for Santa Claus. It was an elf chair. And on the arm of it was a napkin and a coaster and an empty glass.

As Geimle turned to Karble he heard heavy footsteps on the bare wood floors. He processed everything at once. There was no Big Guy—not in this room. Probably not in the castle.

"You were listening in," he said to Karble. "How long have you been sitting up here in his bedroom, watching?"

Before she could answer, Ma Claus, breathless, showed up in the doorway and offered Geimle hot chocolate and a slice of pie.

He was right, she told him. Santa was gone, he was told. They were sitting at the table in the sunroom. Ma Claus told him he'd been gone for weeks. Yes, he had been sick when he first got back. It had been pretty bad. But he'd recovered from that months ago—at least the physical part. He'd made the mistake, she said, of wondering how everything was getting on without him. That's when he'd asked Karble to install the monitors in his sickroom and all over the North Pole.

"He followed everything," Karble said. "He's really quite amazing. He knew everything that was going on in the factory and everywhere. You think he's not paying attention, that he's missing important things. But he's not. He doesn't miss anything."

"Everywhere?" said Geimle.

"Everywhere there was work being done," said Ma.

"So he knew about my plan, and the missing deer, and…?"

"Even Motto and Botto and me and Gully. He knew everything. I could fool Haymin. His security isn't half as good as he thinks it is. But I couldn't fool the Big Guy," said Karble.

"He was full of compliments for everyone. He thought you were doing a bang-up job," said Ma.

"But he was also kind of sad," said Minina. "And he wouldn't tell us why."

"Not even me," said Ma. "Whenever I asked him, he said, 'no, no, no, not sad. Just serious."

"For the Big Guy, anything less than jolly would look sad," said Geimle.

"He was definitely not jolly," said Karble.

"And then he left. Karble got him a deer and an old colly-bird sleigh they used for training young reindeer and he took off."

"It wasn't hard," said Karble. "He said he thought he'd heal better down there."

"Yes, but mostly he said he had some thinking to do," said Ma Claus. "I think that's the real reason he went away."

"Should we be worried?" said Geimle.

"No, I don't think so," said Ma Claus. "Not too worried. He calls almost every day or I call him. He seems fine."

"Says he's getting stronger all the time," said Karble.

"Doesn't say what he's thinking about however," said Ma Claus, "or what he's doing."

"He did say," Minina said, "he did say things up here were going just as smoothly as if he was supervising himself. Karble sends him reports every day."

"And he can watch everything from his phone too," Karble added.

"It's September," said Geimle, "the busy time. He must be coming back soon."

Minina said, "I don't think so. Maybe not. He said everyone was doing such a fine job, he wasn't needed until Christmas Eve—if then."

"He's not feeling useless, I hope, not the Big Guy."

"No, I don't think it's that," said Ma Claus. "I think he's proud of how well the operation is running without him."

"But it's not," said Geimle. "It's not running well at all. We're bleeding elves. I don't know if we'll even be ready for Christmas.

It's...it's...it's hard. It's never been like this before. And it's been like that all year. How could he say we're doing well?"

"He thinks you're doing very well," said Karble.

"Next time he calls, you tell him to come right back, right away," said Geimle.

41

CLAIRE'S DOOR WAS LOCKED again as soon as she returned, which was not long after Flossie landed and took after Comet and the elves for home. After all that flying, Botto and Gully trusted the girls and the reindeer to make it safely from Minnesota to Indiana without them. And Flossie certainly knew her way to the North Pole.

Claire did not return from California happy. When she wasn't working in her office she was complaining about the lack of support she got around the house with the laundry and the meals and the cleaning. "You're all three old enough to start doing some work around here," she said. And even to Morris' dad she said, "Just because I'm the woman doesn't mean all the cleaning is always up to me."

"But we're doing everything the same as always," said Morris. "Why all of a sudden is she bitching about it?"

"Mark Tortare's house," said Jasmine. "Lord & Taylor. That's incompatible with... with just plain messy."

"Maybe he just called it off. Maybe she's angry about that."

"Yeah, but that would be good," said Tanya.

There were loud discussions in the parents' bedroom too. The children couldn't quite make out all the words, and they didn't sound really angry—no one was yelling exactly—but they the emotion was high on both sides. Morris' dad would say things like,

"It doesn't matter." And Claire would say things like, "It's just everything."

There was no way to know what story Claire was telling him or what he thought he knew.

For the children, the real question hadn't changed: was Claire going away? And would she take Tanya and Jasmine with her if she did? And what about Morris and his dad? They felt helpless. They'd gathered a lot of information, and it didn't lead to any certain conclusion and even if it did there wasn't much they could do about it.

The envelope with the birth certificate arrived in the mail two days after Claire got home. Morris saw it in a pile of mail. But by the time he'd gone down the hallway to get Jasmine to pick it up and bring it to her mother and ask her about it, Claire had come across it, and it was gone. No one could figure out how to ask about something they weren't supposed to have seen, but Jasmine did her best.

"Why would you be getting mail from a hospital in California?" she asked.

Claire tightened her grip on her mug of tea. Her head jerked toward Jasmine as though they were turning toward a sudden movement out the corner her eye.

"Why you asking that?"

"Morris said he saw an envelope from a children's hospital or something."

She composed herself quickly. "Just something for my book." And then she added immediately, "That's a very strange question."

"He just mentioned it, no big deal." They had to let the topic drop because they couldn't think of any way to keep it going. And Jasmine convinced Tanya and Morris that they'd made Claire suspicious. And even if they could get her to lose that suspicion, how could they possibly ask her about Tiara Williams? Tanya just wanted to go up and blurt it out and confess everything. But that, or anything they might do to stop her from leaving, might just as well push her away out of annoyance.

Tanya decided that their mother wanted to leave, but that Mark Tortare wouldn't take her and Jasmine, and so she had to choose between them. And that's what she was trying to do now. And that's what made her so cranky. Jasmine thought she wanted to leave the girls behind but was waiting to make sure Morris' dad would take them and raise them so they wouldn't have to become wards of the state—which, if he would take them, all that would really mean would be just letting them continue to live here in the house because "parenting" wasn't something he really did, not even with Morris. But Morris' dad was probably holding out on agreeing because he didn't want Claire to leave. As the weeks passed and Claire stayed nervous or angry a lot of the time, Morris decided she'd had to give up on the California dream, probably because of the kids, probably because Mark learned about them and just dumped her. Wouldn't she have left by now if she was going?

The girls couldn't say.

It all came back to the holes in their information. They were not able to uncover anything more of Claire's communications with California or anything more about Mark Tortare or even Willard Tremont, who didn't want to talk to them anymore, which meant that he might still be more involved than he'd let on. But Claire did do something, finally, that amounted to a clue.

She made a pot roast. And she baked potatoes and steamed a great big pot of green beans she'd bought at the grocery store that day. And everyone sat down at the same hour at the same table to eat dinner. *That* was something that never happened in this house. Claire was not fond of cooking. Anyone who knew her knew that.

And Morris' dad never cooked. He just warmed things up that came in packages. Morris and Jasmine and Tanya sometimes ate together in the evening. They would search the cupboards and pantry when one of them got hungry and see what they could come up with. A lot of times it was whole wheat spaghetti with canned sauce. Then the three of them would sit together at the table or around the TV and try to work out in conspiratorial tones what was happening between Claire and California. But the lack of evidence always lead the conversation to meander like the monologue of a drunk comedian. And the longer Claire stayed in Indiana the more convinced they were that whatever had happened last summer was over. They'd probably never find out the details. But somehow she'd tried out California and it hadn't worked out, and that was that, and for the foreseeable future this was their lives. And that was okay. Sometimes when they had nothing new to say, Jasmine would bring out songs she'd play on her guitar and give the lyrics to Morris and Tanya to sing. Most of the time they wandered away to hang out with their various friends or do homework.

Morris and Jasmine continued a habit they'd begun when they first met the elves and took long bike trips together. They were getting along very well. Having no biological parents in common, they were becoming friends. They noticed it, but they didn't talk about it. They all thought it was very nice—and then they realized it was a problem, perhaps a fatal one.

On the day she served the pot roast, Claire said, trying to sound conversational, "We've noticed how well you three have been getting along."

Morris said, "Well Jasmine's come a long way on that guitar."

And Tanya said, "It's nice that Morris doesn't spend absolutely all his time playing video games."

Then Morris' dad said, "And you've gone a long way on that bike. Where do you go?"

"Just around," said Jasmine. "It's good exercise."

Then Claire said, "It would be a shame to break up such a tight gang."

The kids went silent and just looked at each other.

Tanya said later that she probably should have said something at that moment, something like "why would that happen?" But after a few minutes of silence, it seemed like the window for such a comment had shut. She'd been waiting for someone else to say something.

What did it mean? Jasmine said it could only be one thing: the California scheme was not over. Claire *was* going to leave. She was going to leave her daughters in Indiana, and she was saying good-bye with this nice meal. Any day they'd wake up and find another note on the table, and that would be that. Tanya thought it was time to confront her. Jasmine and Morris reminded her again how bad that had gone last time and that it would just make her angry.

Gully agreed with Morris and Jasmine. They had of course kept their elf friends up to date on everything. "I like subtle," she texted. "Ask about the snow globe."

"Whatever happened to that snow globe," Jasmine asked her mother the next chance she got.

Claire looked surprised. But she pretended not to understand. "What snow globe?"

What she wanted to say was, "You know, the one you gave to Willard Tremont that magically showed up at Mark Tortare's house?" But instead she said, "The one Morris and I got you last summer."

"The thing you swiped from the garbage can? I don't know. I probably threw it away."

Tanya piped up at that: "You wouldn't throw away something that's worth a hundred dollars."

Claire seemed to be knocked a little off balance. But she caught herself immediately, "No, I suppose I wouldn't," she said. "Must be in my office somewhere. Why do you want to know?"

Now it was the girls' turn to wobble. They hadn't anticipated the question, although they realized afterwards that it was a pretty obvious question. But Morris called from the kitchen table where he was eating a large bowl of cereal: "We were hoping to sell it. If you didn't want it, like it looked like you didn't, we could put it on eBay."

"Oh, I don't know," said Claire. "You give me a gift and then you want to take it away?"

"But if you don't want it," said Jasmine.

"I don't even know where it is."

"We'll look for it," said Tanya. "Your office isn't that big."

Once again Claire stumbled searching for a response.

"Unless you left it in California," Morris called over.

"Why would I go and take a snow globe to California?"

"Maybe that *is* what you did," said Jasmine.

"Who's in California that you'd give a hundred dollar gift to?" said Tanya, no longer sure this conversation could be classified as subtle.

"It's not like it *cost* anyone a hundred dollars," said Claire. "You found it on a trash can."

"But who'd you give it to?" said Morris.

Claire placed both palms flat on the counter and leaned over. "The agent," she said. "I remember. I thought it would be a good idea to give him something special for looking at my book."

"That sounds weird," said Tanya. She expected to get yelled at for disrespectful language. But that's not what happened. Claire got flustered.

"Look, I don't need any of this interrogation from you. What you need money for anyway?"

That was another question they had not anticipated. But Morris had an answer as good and as quick as any they could have planned.

"Christmas presents," he said.

"Already?"

"I like to be prepared." Morris knew how unconvincing that sounded in October, but Claire let it go.

"Well, you'll just have to sell some of those useless old video games, I guess." Morris couldn't tell if she was calling all video games useless or just noting that there must be some he didn't ever play anymore. "Too damn clever for your own good," she said, "I don't know why I put up with you anyway." And then she headed down to her office.

That sounded ominous.

They called Gully right away. "We did what you suggested."

"And what did you learn?"

"I don't think we learned anything."

"I think she learned something," said Tanya.

Gully asked them to tell her exactly what happened, what everyone said.

"Okay," she said, "this is what you learned: you learned that she knows you're on to her. That's good."

"Is it going to stop her?"

"I doubt it. Sounds like she's just about ready to make her move. But at least it might get it all out in the open."

"Why don't *we* get it out in the open?"

"She'll just deny it. Trust me, you need to be careful. You just blurt things out, that could be dangerous. She needs to be ready to talk about it or it'll just be a shouting match—which you would lose—and which would make her angry, and that'll definitely drive her away. But you did okay. You just let her know it's time to be ready to talk about it, so she'd better hop on her reindeer and start talking."

That sounded reasonable, except for the part about the reindeer.

"By tomorrow, you'll have the whole story. I guarantee it."

But that's not what happened. Weeks went by. Halloween and Thanksgiving came and went, and Claire didn't say or do anything. The kids could only believe something had gone wrong again with the California idea, and maybe when she said "It would be a shame to break you up," what she meant was that she was going to stay in Indiana because she couldn't stand to go to California without Jasmine and Tanya. So instead of meaning, "I'm going to go to California without you," she meant, "I'm not going to go to California after all." And maybe when she said, "I don't know why I put up with you," she didn't mean she wasn't going to do it anymore but that she was going to stay and find out.

Or maybe she was just waiting till after Christmas. Were the secret lives of parents this complicated in every house?

The Christmas decorations went up. And everything about California was receding into whatever that place might be where dreams go when you wake up. Now Claire was happy almost all the time. She gave the kids money to buy presents. She worked up plans for a big Christmas dinner. Jasmine worked up some songs for everyone to learn and perform, and Claire said she had a surprise.

And then she was gone. Nothing happened. No one was yelling or fighting. She just wrote one of her enigmatic notes, dropped it on the kitchen table among the packages of unhung tinsel and took off.

42

"DOING HOMEWORK TOGETHER? All three of you. How nice." Morris' dad pulled open the junk mail drawer and dropped the day's pile on top of all the other unopened mail. He always planned to take the time to go through all that junk in case there was something important. But that event never seemed urgent enough to actually happen. Two or three times a year, he'd look at all the unopened mail and announce, with a chuckle, "if there was anything here that mattered, I'd've heard about it by now," and he'd cast the whole lot into recycle. It was like a ritual. When he was younger, Morris sometimes went through all the tossed mail looking for treasure— mostly stickers and magnets but also sometimes nickels and quarters and now and then even a crisp dollar bill sent by a charity to induce business.

Morris' dad patted his son on the back and went upstairs.

The children's cell phones were propped in front of them. They were staring intently and writing things on pieces of paper.

"He thought this was homework?" came Gullnle's voice from Jasmine's phone.

"You guys do homework with your phones?" came Botto's voice from Morris' phone.

"I do not think that's such a good idea," came Motto's voice from Tanya's phone.

"Hey, what's with the mail?" Botto was having trouble focusing on the problem. "Boy, if we did that with our mail, there'd be tears at Christmas from Beijing to Fresno."

"It's just junk," said Morris.

"We should have confronted mom when we had the chance." Jasmine wanted to bring everyone back to the topic.

"That would've just made her angry," said Tanya.

"She left anyway," said Jasmine.

"But then you would've blamed yourselves," said Motto.

"It doesn't matter what you might have done," said Gullnle. "Time won't ever go backwards. I say you confront her now."

"She won't answer her phone," said Morris. "It's not even turned on."

"Then you've got to go back to California," said Gullnle.

"How are they going to go to California? The door of the vortex is in Saskatchewan," said Motto.

"That wouldn't matter anyway," said Karble through Tanya's phone. "You can't confront someone inside the vortex. Try Facebook."

"Seriously?" said Jasmine.

"No, no, no. They need to take a plane," said Gullnle. It's gotta be face-to-face. It's too late for this subtlety garbage."

"On their own?" said Botto. "They're just kids. We sure can't get there to help. Any of you been near the reindeer fortress lately?"

"That's true," said Gully to the kids. "Haymin's got spiked fences and armed guards."

"He does not," said Motto.

"I think it was a figure of speech," said Botto.

"Right. The one they call 'lying,'" Motto chuckled.

"Hey!" said Gullnle, but she also chuckled.

"So they'll just have to go on their own," said Botto.

"You want kids running around the country without supervision?" said Karble.

"They're big kids," said Gully.

"Well it doesn't matter because we don't have a plane," said Morris.

"Don't they have airports in Indiana?" said Gully.

"Where are we going to get the money for the tickets?" said Tanya.

"It's not a good idea anyway," said Karble. "Just forget it."

"Yeah, that really might not be the best," said Motto.

"Unless," said Morris. And a smirk bloomed on his face as he slid over to the mail drawer and pulled out piles and piles of envelopes. "There's usually credit cards in some of these."

"I don't know," said Jasmine.

"Plane tickets are expensive," said Tanya.

"Right. We might need more than one," said Morris, and he passed piles of junk mail to each of them.

"Oh, that is such a bad idea," said Karble, "in so many ways."

There were four unactivated credit cards among the junk. One was Claire's.

"She'll kill us," said Jasmine. "And so will your dad."

"She'll have to come home first to do that," Tanya said. "Look, we've been doing nothing for months because we're scared what will happen—and look what happened."

"Really not a good idea," said Karble.

"We'll call you back," said Tanya. And they disconnected.

The plan worked surprisingly easy from the start. They decided to start with Claire's card. But they didn't just activate it. They changed the mailing address so the bill would not come to Indiana. It would go to Mark Tortare's house. Then Tanya called the limo company. She paid online so there was no messy conversation with the driver. When the van arrived at the house, everyone just piled in with their backpacks. They kept thinking someone was going to see three children traveling alone, but no one questioned it. Gullnle called Tanya before they left: "Just do the elf thing—act like nothing's wrong and mostly likely no one will notice."

They printed their boarding passes at home and their backpacks were carry-ons, so there was very little contact with anyone at the airport. The website told them to get there two hours early, so they did. But there didn't seem to be any reason for that. The terminal was crowded at first, but a plane landed at their gate and all the people cleared out. Jasmine felt exposed and nervous. If someone was looking for three kids traveling alone together—like if Morris' dad somehow figured out they were gone and called the police and put out a search—they'd be pretty easy to spot. It wasn't likely. Morris reminded her it was a good plan if they stuck to it. But if, like Gully said, people won't notice unless you give them a reason to, well, acting nervous was a reason. Jasmine agreed. But she was nervous anyway.

Karble called Tanya and offered to help.

"Gully's already helping."

"Do you want to end up in California or Abu Dhabi?"

"I thought you didn't want us to do this."

"I don't. You're just kids. But you're obviously doing it. I can't stop you. So I'm going to try to help you."

"Jasmine's afraid."

"So put her on."

Karble told Jasmine to use her headphones so people wouldn't overhear and to casually walk around the room with the camera on, as though she were having a private conversation. Karble wanted to get the lay of the room. There was no one there besides the woman at the counter and an old man who was nodding off in one of the chairs.

"The woman behind the counter is watching us," said Jasmine. She pointed the camera her way.

The young woman at the ticket desk looked over. Then she looked down at her computer screen. But then she looked over again.

"Maybe," said Karble. "But I don't think so. I don't think she's suspicious. But let's be sure." She told her to gather the others and get their stuff and just go for a walk. "Look purposeful," she said.

"I don't want to be walking these hallways for two hours," said Tanya after their second newsstand.

"Maybe there's more people at the terminal by now," said Karble.

But there weren't many, just that old man who was now awake and a mother with three children frantically engaging the boarding clerk.

"Sit behind the old man," said Karble. "He'll block the view."

They made a wall with their backs.

It wasn't long before Tanya said, "Don't you keep looking over there." Jasmine kept shifting her gaze suspiciously to the desk where the mother was still in deep dispute with the clerk. More people filtered into the room.

And then the three little children left their mother and ran up to the old man that they were using to block the view. The children came to a rapid stop in front of the old man and started giggling. The old man waved and giggled back. The young mother left her papers on the desk and charged into the scene, drawing everyone's eyes right in the direction of Jasmine, Tanya, and Morris. The mother was yelling, "Come here, you leave that man alone." She apologized to the old man. Jasmine and Tanya and Morris stiffened their backs and listened.

One of the kids said, "I want a 'intendo." And the old man said, "No problem ma'am. Happens all the time. Price of wearing a beard at my age," and he laughed. Jasmine turned her head sideways to peek.

The woman tried to shoo her kids away from the old man but the giggling girl sat down on the seat beside him and made herself heavy and her two brothers flanked him. One of them tried to climb up on his knees. Tanya hit Jasmine on the leg to get her to look away. But Jasmine ignored her. Then Morris turned his head and watched too.

"I think you need to go with your mother," the old man said. And he put his hand in his pocket pulled out three little plastic-wrapped items and offered them to the woman and winked.

"I don't think we should reward them for bad behavior," said the woman.

"You're the mother," said the old man, and he put two of the items back in his pocket, saying, "Now, go with your mother, children."

Tanya turned her head and watched the mother drag the kids away in tears.

When they were gone, the old man opened the package and put a little plastic flute to his lips and blew. It made a soft, musical sound and filled the air around him with soap bubbles. "She should have taken it. You'd be surprised how effective a toy flute that blows soap bubbles can be for delaying tears." He spoke these words to no one in particular, unless there were an invisible someone standing beside him.

During all this, more people had been coming in and taking seats at the gate, which was now half full. Jasmine, Tanya, and Morris felt a little safer from detection.

When the time came, they handed their boarding passes to the gatekeeper, and she let them on the plane. Just like that. Tanya took the window seat. Morris took the aisle. They didn't say much. They were trying to be invisible. The old man from the gate pushed down the aisle and took the seat across from Morris. He was a little chubby, and he had a white beard. It wasn't really a long beard, but it was understandable that little kids would take him for Santa Claus.

"Excuse me," he said to Morris, "might I push your backpack to the side a bit so I can slip my valise in this bin?"

This was Morris' first plane ride. He didn't know the protocols. "Yeah, go ahead."

"Much obliged," he said. That was not a phrase Morris was familiar with.

The old man sat down across the aisle. He chose the nearest seat, leaving the other two empty on his side of the plane. "I noticed you three are traveling alone," he said as he sat down. "Meeting someone?"

Morris immediately decided he was a creep. "Yeah, he said. My dad. He's a cop. He'll just be getting off his shift. Probably come with his gun and everything."

The old man laughed. "Very good," he said. "I would have expected no less. Name's Good," he said, "Sam Good." And the old man reached his hand across the aisle to shake Morris'. Morris just stared at the hand. He didn't know what to do. But then more people pushed by and Sam Good was forced to withdraw.

"No," said Sam, looking forward but still talking to Morris. Jasmine and Tanya by this time had turned their heads to watch.

"Of course, you should be wary. Children traveling alone, accosted by a talkative old man." Then he turned his head back in Morris direction. "Hello, Tanya, Jasmine."

"What?" said Jasmine.

"He obviously heard our names back in the gate. He was sitting right behind us."

"That's right," said Sam Good. "Quite wary. That's good. Just so you know, very talkative but completely harmless, especially when I'm nervous. And I must say, flying makes me nervous." And then he reached into his pocket and pulled out three more of his bubble blowing flutes and handed them across the aisle to Morris. Morris hesitated again, but the old man said, "Really, there's caution and there's caution. They're fun, and a good distraction if you get nervous on the way up or the way down—until someone complains about the bubbles of course." Morris didn't want to look like a coward. He took them. One was white, one yellow, one brown. They were still in their packaging. He kept the brown one.

"Friend of mine designed them. I plan to pitch them to a buyer in Los Angeles. Curious what you think," he said. But just then his phone rang. He stuck an ear bud in his ear and turned his full attention to his new conversation. The children watched the people file on the plane and the carts zip around on the tarmac with the luggage and the woman with the orange flashlights and they forgot about Sam Good until they were airborne. The battery went dead on Morris' phone. He had to put it away. He couldn't play any more games, and he hadn't brought anything else to do.

"I thought they showed movies," he was talking to Jasmine, but Sam Good answered.

"So did I," he said. "Apparently not on these short, domestic excursions. I see no advantage to airplanes."

"They're faster," said Morris.

"Faster than what?" said Sam Good. He turned his head toward Morris like a patient on a bed, without the rest of his body shifting, and the look on his face was not creepy at all. It was friendly.

"Why would you want to look like Santa Claus?" said Morris.

"I work in toys," he said.

Morris imagined he did his own commercials like those CEOs from car companies. He could see how that would be helpful.

Sam said, "I noticed you didn't try the flutes."

"We kinda don't want…"

"You don't want to draw the attention of the attendants. Any more cautious and you never would have let yourselves onto a plane."

Sam Good reclined his torso in his seat, which was uncomfortably small for him. He was a pretty large man. He pressed the button for the flight attendant and pulled an envelope from his vest pocket.

"I wonder if it's possible I have been incorrectly seated," he said when the attendant arrived.

"Oh, my goodness," said the attendant. "You're in first class. This is coach."

Two attendants led Sam Good and his bag though the curtain.

"That's just plain weird," said Morris.

"What is?" Jasmine looked up from her phone.

"How could a guy not know he's not in first class?"

"Maybe he's never flown before."

"*I've* never flown before," said Morris.

A minute later one of the attendants who had led Sam Good away came up to the children and asked if they would care to join their uncle in first class.

"No," said Jasmine immediately.

"You nuts?" Morris had talked to him enough by now to decide he was just who he said he was: a harmless old man who sold toys and didn't like airplanes.

"Uncle who?" said Tanya who had been staring out the window ever since take off.

"He's a stranger," said Jasmine.

"We're in an airplane. And we're not little kids," said Morris. "And there are three of us. And he's old."

Morris got up. "Lead the way," he said to the confused attendant. He waved his stepsisters to follow.

"What if really he is, you know, Botto's actual boss?" Jasmine said to Morris over his shoulder.

Morris scoffed. "Yeah, on a plane?"

"Would someone tell me where we're going?" said Tanya.

Morris grabbed Jasmine's phone and fiddled around on the screen as the flight attendant led them toward the barrier separating coach from the forward areas of the plane. Just before they crossed, Morris held the results of his search in front of her face: *The Fraternal Order of Real Bearded Santas*. "There's hundreds of guys out there that look like that."

She pulled the phone back and Tanya reached forward to see what she was looking at.

"It's a club for old guys with nothing better to do."

The attendant led the children forward through the wide seats of business class and up to the plush leather of first class.

Sam Good sat in a group of four seats that were arranged to face each other. There was no one else in this section of the plane. Either Mr. Good had bought out every seat in first class or there just weren't any rich people flying to California today. He put his flute to his lips and blew a soft musical tune as the children entered; soap bubbles rose from the tip of the flute and circled his head like smoke.

"You can blow bubbles to your heart's content up here," he said. "What do you think?"

"Why are you the only one?" said Jasmine.

"I might have hit that 'purchase' button too many times," he chuckled. "Have you ever noticed: computers—I've never taken to them—they always do what they think you want. They never do what you actually want. Good invention, I guess, if they can ever get it ready to market." He passed around a basket full of soft drinks and snacks.

None of the children tried out the bubble flute. Sam Good did not seem to notice. He seemed to have brought the three of them to join him just for someone to talk to. He wanted to know all about them: what they hoped for in life, what their interests were in school, what they thought the advantages were of a mixed and blended family, what they wanted for Christmas, what they thought of flying, what their favorite games were, what they wanted to be when they grew up, and did they really want to grow up if they had a choice in the matter? He seemed to enjoy chuckling and he didn't seem to be asking the questions just to avoid the awkwardness of silence. He really wanted to know the answers. The children were comfortable almost immediately, especially as it became clear that there were questions he was not going to ask: such as where were they going, why were they traveling together, and why was there no adult with them? And that was good because each one realized they hadn't rehearsed answers to these questions.

It was a long time before the conversation wound its way back to the flute.

"You don't think kids will like your flute?" said Morris.

"I don't think they'll ever get to find out," said Sam. "Physical toys—it's a retrograde affair. Market's shrinking year by year along with my company." And he chuckled again. It did not seem like a nervous chuckle but a genuinely happy laugh, as though he'd just seen something amusing and unexpected. "Just look at all of you: phone, phone, phone."

"You don't seem unhappy about it," said Tanya.

"Should I be?"

"Your company," said Jasmine. "And the children."

"Well, I do feel bad for the children. I'm not against video toys," he said. "Material for the imagination. But the physical toys that make you run around, that make your parents shoo you outside so you don't make a mess, make you have to shift gravity and turn trees into sheriffs and aliens, and alien sheriffs, you invent a whole world out of nothing on the fly like little gods. Wouldn't want to lose that."

The children didn't know what to say.

"But what can I do? I'm thinking it may be time to pack it in for good."

"You're gonna sell your business?" asked Jasmine.

"Oh, I doubt it. No, I may just dissolve the company altogether."

"But you're not upset?" said Morris. "Why not?"

Sam Good laughed loudly. And he spread his arms out as though he were trying to wrap them around the plane and give it a hug. "How much time do we have?" But he didn't wait for an answer. "The world will get by without my business. I'll tell you this, people who try to adjust the knobs on the world, who won't be happy until they've converted everything and everyone into what they think they want or how they think things are supposed to be— those are unhappy people. They've lost before they've even started. When the time comes to let go, let go."

"But how do you know when that time is?" said Jasmine.

"Yes, that's the trick," he said. "It's like.... We have this kind of rose where I come from. It grows backwards. It's a beautiful, beautiful flower. You plant it and in a couple years it becomes an extraordinary bush." He held out his hands to indicate the size. "And then the next year, it comes back a little smaller. Packed with blossoms. You just have to trim away the dead stalks. And the next year, it's even smaller. And it grows smaller and smaller every year after that. There's nothing amiss. That's just how it works. It's backwards from every other kind of plant. It doesn't matter what you do. You can fertilize it, pollinate it, pray over it, talk its ear off, it just grows smaller every year until one year it doesn't come back at all."

"But a new flower takes its place," said Tanya.

"No, it's just a dead stalk with hard little thorns on it. But some of them, some of them drop a seed in their last year. Otherwise, you can't know it's over until it's over."

"But some things aren't supposed to change," Tanya erupted. "When things break, when they aren't working like they're supposed to, you have to fix them."

Sam Good did not laugh. "Go ahead, play your flutes. I want to know what you think."

And it seemed to each of the children that the future of Sam Good's toy business might depend on what happened next. Would these three kids on this one plane who had more than enough to distract them from playing with toys right now enjoy them? The children lifted their flutes to give them a look. Jasmine blew on hers and quickly figured out where the notes were. Tanya said, "I'm not very good with musical instruments."

"Oh, you don't have to be," said Sam. And he turned his flute over. "There's a chip inside. Slide the switch here, you just have to blow, and it'll play a song for you. Put it here, and you can use it like a regular flute. That's the default. And this one here turns the bubbles on. Is that too complicated for a toy? Because I actually wanted to add colored lights inside the fuselage here so it would change color with the note. You can also turn off the music and just blow bubbles. And if you know what you're doing," Sam Good flicked the switch and held a button and let the flute play *Green Sleeves* and blow bubbles without holding it to his lips. "Listen to that. Isn't that a beautiful tune? You're welcome to be sad whenever that ends," he chuckled. His face beamed and he seemed to be holding back a laugh so that the notes of the laugh wouldn't ruin the song. The song wound through two verses and into the third and then, abruptly, it stopped. Sam Good shook the toy. "Well that's frustrating." He slipped the flute into his pocket with a frown.

43

SAM GOOD GOT UP WHEN THE PLANE STOPPED in Phoenix to take on new passengers. He must have got off because when the plane pulled back onto the runway, he wasn't there. A few people filed into first class. But no one told the children they had to move.

They took a bus to Yorba Linda, then a cab to Mark Tortare's neighborhood. They had the driver stop at the end of the road so they could walk. They wanted to approach the house slowly—and they didn't want anyone who happened to be standing by a window to see them getting out of a taxi.

Being in this place, where every house verged on Lord &Taylor, in real time, was different from being here in the vortex. It was almost like the difference between wearing a costume in a play, where it fit in, and wearing that same costume later in a restaurant for the cast party where all the other customers stared. For Morris, who'd seen the neighborhood only from satellite pictures, that difference didn't register, but still, it didn't smell or look like anything he knew in Indiana. He'd expected, from the pictures he'd seen, that it would look like a studio backdrop for a movie. And it did look like it was trying to look like that. But now that he was here, what he noticed were the signs of real people's actual lives— like the car parked on the road that blocked the view of an elaborate Christmas display, or the tall stockade fence that ran alongside the short split-rail fence that hinted that one neighbor was trying to block out the style choice of the other.

But those signs would blur and fade real soon when the sun set and the Christmas lights came on. In fact some of them were already on. One palm tree had lights all the way to the top. Soon this place would look a lot like a Christmas card, with spotlights illuminating yard décor. Almost every yard had something, a manger scene or a Santa Claus (and not one of those inflatable ones like they had around his house). In one yard, the manger scene was almost big enough for real people, and behind it was a ten-foot Christmas tree with boxes of presents big enough to fit a whole Christmas morning inside each one. A sleigh with the reindeer was across the street from Mark Tortare's house. Inside it sat a stuffed Saint Nick and a couple of elves that looked like they were made of foam. It was decked out in black and gold and the reindeer were animatronic, bobbing their heads. It was very stagey; it was Lord & Taylor, military neat. But still they could all see why someone would want to live here, why a certain kind of person might be tempted to give up on Indiana for a place like this.

The children all had the same feeling of not knowing what to do next. They hadn't planned the encounter out in detail. They just knew they wanted to confront Claire and her boyfriend in this place where she couldn't deny it or make up stories about what was going on. They talked about just waltzing in and pretending they already lived here. But what might be good for a laugh in a movie wouldn't necessarily work in real life. No, they'd probably just have to knock on the door and say, "Is mom here?" and then just let what happened next happen.

"Maybe when he meets us, he'll want us too," said Tanya.

"Until he gets the bill," said Morris.

That was followed by silence.

"She can't keep doing this to you," Morris said. "Do you want to be dragged here to this nice house and then dragged to, I don't know, like Michigan or something next year?"

"Maybe I'll just go around the back and peek in the window," Tanya said, "see what they might be up to." She looked around for anyone watching, then stole along the fence.

Morris and Jasmine stopped. A street lamp flickered and came on. It didn't seem to add light anywhere near the ground. Although it was still fairly bright outside, inside the houses, lights were starting to burn in the windows and some of the colored lights that framed the houses and bushes came on. At the property line by a stand of palm trees, they watched two children in Mark Tartare's driveway, two little girls beside a parked tricycle and a bike with training wheels. The girls were drawing on the pavement with chalk, oblivious to the whole world.

"Mom used to give us chalk when she wanted to get rid of us," said Jasmine. "'Here, got you some more chalk. Draw me a picture.'"

Mark Tortare's girls had drawn very elaborate, very colorful pictures of giant flowers and small houses and fairies flying around.

"That's very pretty," said Jasmine, nodding toward the blue sun glowing over the orange field and the yellow ocean. "Why is it blue?"

The little girl looked up then looked back at the drawing. "Because it's night time," she said.

"Some suns are blue," said her sister.

"Where'd you get the chalk?" said Jasmine.

The older girl took a step back and stared suspiciously.

"Aunt Claire," said the younger girl.

"Is Aunt Claire here?" said Morris. He got no answer.

"Can I draw too?" Jasmine squatted and reached her hand out for some chalk.

"Daddy said…" said the older girl. "You're strangers."

"Aunt Claire used to give me chalk all the time," she said. "What if I put a whale in the ocean?"

Jasmine drew a quick whale and the younger sister scribbled water shooting from its spout.

"You know Aunt Claire?" said the older girl.

"Oh, sure," said Jasmine. "I came to see her."

"Is Aunt Claire inside?" said Morris again.

"So Aunt Claire is good to you," said Jasmine. "She was good to me too."

"She bought us bikes for Christmas," said the older girl.

"But it isn't Christmas yet," said Morris.

"She can't be here for Christmas."

Just then the front door burst open and a man charged out, yelling, "Hey, you. What the hell are you doing? Girls, come here, right now."

Jasmine dropped the chalk and bolted up.

"We're just going for a walk, sir. We're just talking," said Morris. By then the man—he looked just like he did on Facebook— was hovering over both of them. He was thin and tall and still in his suit from his work day. He had a gold stub in his left ear. He pointed to his girls and then to the house. They dropped their chalk and marched inside.

"You live around here? You visiting someone? You don't live on this street."

"No, sir, we don't," said Morris.

"We just… I was just…" Jasmine didn't know exactly what she wanted to say. "We were just walking."

"Well you just keep walking." But then his tone shifted ever so slightly, "I'm sorry. I don't know you. You're not from here. You just need to keep walking."

Tanya came a step around the corner of the house. Morris and Jasmine both saw her. She stared over just as Mark Tortare was raising his finger to point them the way to the end of the street. Tanya moved to hide herself around the corner of his house, but just as she was doing this, Mark Tortare, seeing where Morris and Jasmine were looking, turned in her direction. He glanced back at Jasmine and Morris, then back to where Tanya had been, yelled "HEY!" and took off after her with three long strides before breaking into a run.

Jasmine bolted after. Morris hesitated just a second then took off as well. Jasmine rounded the corner first. She saw Tanya standing with her back against a fence and Mark Tortare closing in. And then she saw Mark Tortare hurtling toward the ground as though he had been tripped. One second later, when Morris arrived, Mark Tortare in his pretty lawyer suit was lying splat on the grass. By his foot on the lawn was a lump of something. Tanya sprinted toward the front of the house. Before Mark Tortare could get up or Jasmine and Morris could turn around the words "climb in" came from over their shoulders. And there behind them was the sleigh from the display across the street. And Tanya was in it. And so were Karble and Gullnle and a stuffed Santa. "Quick," they said.

In another moment, they were flying.

44

"WHAT JUST HAPPENED?" They had just cleared the tree across the street. Jasmine was staring back over the roof of the house. Mark Tortare was rushing around, clearly looking for Tanya—everywhere but up.

"Botto tripped him," said Gully. "You're lucky. That guy had murder in his eyes."

"He did not," said Morris. "He was just looking out for his kids."

"Botto? What was he, invisible?" said Jasmine.

"I didn't see him," said Morris.

"No, no. He was inside the vortex," said Karble. "We had him standing by, just in case."

"No, no, no," Morris knew the vortex better than that. "That can't work."

But it can, Karble told them. And it did. Botto had been stationed right by the vortex door, just in case. Fortunately, the door to the vortex was now very conveniently just outside the factory at the North Pole. So that part was easy. After their last phone call to the kids, Karble told Gullnle the kids might need help and she knew how to get two reindeer and a sleigh. And that was all Gullnle needed. Karble worked her magic with electronics and cameras and got the transportation past the ever-more-watchful eyes of Haymin and off they flew. It was a great time of year for elves and reindeer to get lost in America. They just blended in as lawn décor. Even the kids hadn't recognized them, though they were staring right at them when they came down the street. They saw everything. The moment Mark Tortare came out of the house, they put Botto into action.

"But all the way from the North Pole? That would take—even on a reindeer..." said Jasmine.

"I'm sure it did," said Karble. "A long time—if you're inside the vortex. By the time he got here, I'm guessing Mark Tortare was already in the backyard. He put something under his foot. That slowed him down."

"It was the snow globe," said Tanya. "It was mom's present."

"But you can't..." said Jasmine.

"Yes, you can, because that was something they brought in through the door," Karble said. "Botto's very clever, really."

"That's brilliant," said Morris.

Karble had the reindeer circle the neighborhood. "So what now?"

"We can take you home, if you like," said Gullnle. "Faster than an airplane."

Morris doubted that.

"What about mom?" said Tanya. "I didn't see her."

"We haven't done what we came to do," said Morris.

"You want to go back and face that ogre—now?" said Gullnle. "These are brave kids."

"I can't believe mom would leave us for him," said Jasmine.

"He was just protecting his kids," said Morris.

"From us? What did he think we were going to do, steal them?"

Jasmine pulled out her phone and sent her mom a text: WHERE R U?

Almost immediately she got a text back. I'M IN THE KITCHEN. WHERE ARE YOU?

"The kitchen?" said Tanya. "What….? Oh, crap."

YOUR HOME?

YOU'RE NOT?

Karble pulled thick coats of wool and cotton from a compartment under the bench on which they were sitting and bundled the kids up good.

"How fast is this thing, really?" said Morris.

45

GEIMLE WAS WAITING AT THE VORTEX door when Botto emerged. Malveno was with him, and so was Haymin. Geimle held his hand out for the vortex key. Haymin took Vixen by the reins.

"Would you believe…?"

"Never mind," said Geimle. "Motto told us all about it."

"Stinker," said Botto.

Motto was waiting in Geimle's office. Muted factory noises came through the walls. Geimle sat Botto beside his friend and offered him a hot chocolate. Malveno pushed aside the potted Burzee rose in the center of the table and slid a plate of cookies toward the two young elves.

"Not poisoned, I hope," Botto joked.

No one laughed.

"Not a good time for jokes," said Malveno.

"I always joke when I'm nervous." Images of exile danced in Botto's head. "I like it here."

"We were just trying to help some children," said Motto.

"Never mind that," said Geimle.

"Never mind that?" Motto was suddenly unsure why he was there.

"I swear that's the last time we'll be sneaking into the vortex," said Botto. "It was an emergency. Karble was just…."

"Never mind that," Geimle repeated.

Motto rubbed his neck. Botto bit the glazed head off a gingerbread reindeer. Geimle raised his hands as though he was trying to grab something only he could see and stared first at one then the other before he let the question drop: "Are you two working with the Big Guy. I mean directly. Did he send you into the vortex?"

Botto stopped chewing.

"The Big Guy?" said Motto.

"We know he's up to something," said Geimle. "And we know he's using junior elves."

"And you think he'd trust us?" Botto resumed chewing.

Motto kicked Botto under the table.

"You can never tell with the Big Guy," Malveno shook his head. "He doesn't think like an elf."

"Well, you understand," Motto said, "we may not be at liberty to disclose…"

"What do you think he's up to?" Botto interrupted.

"Well, that's the thing," said Malveno. "If you don't know, we don't want to say."

"And if we do know?" said Motto.

"We know Karble is in on something," said Malveno.

"And maybe Gullnle," said Geimle.

"But the point is, you're all friends. And you," he pointed to Motto, "Karble's especially sweet on you. She must've said something."

"Well you know," said Botto, but Motto grabbed his forearm to get him to stop.

"Can we have a few minutes to talk, just alone, me and Botto," said Motto.

"No," said Geimle.

"No?"

"You need to just tell us what you know," said Malveno. "We're worried. We don't need stories."

"Yeah, I can tell." Botto had never seen Malveno this humorless.

"Okay," said Motto. "How do you know Karble's up to something?"

Geimle hit a button on the remote that was sitting on his table. On the big screen he flashed footage of Karble and Gully sneaking into the reindeer barn. "Haymin set up a second camera," said Geimle. "He's pretty clever himself." The shot never changed. It showed Gullnle and Karble leading Pacer and Blixem out of the barn and hitching them to a one of the colly-bird sleighs.

"Why didn't you stop them?"

"No one was monitoring the screen at the time," said Haymin. "They got lucky."

"It's nearly Christmas," said Geimle. "And they took one of the principle reindeer. Ma Claus said she doesn't know what Karble is up to. The Big Guy won't answer her texts. No one knows where he is. We don't know what to do. So we're hoping you know something we don't."

"You mean in case he doesn't come back in time for delivery?" said Motto.

"What do we do? Go without him? And even if we do? What's next?"

"Is this the end?" said Geimle.

"Why would it be the end?" said Botto.

But before anyone could ask, Motto said, "It might help if you told us what you think is going on."

Geimle sat back. "What I think? All right. It's this: I think we had it figured out all along, really. We were losing control of Christmas. The Big Guy knew it, and he was thinking, 'What would happen if I just gave up? Would anything change?' My plan was right. My plan was too late. It was already too late before I even thought it up, before you two…" Geimle exhaled as though he were releasing pressure from a steam valve, "messed it up. But I'm guessing he told you to do that. That makes sense now. Two junior elves wouldn't just take it upon themselves to steal reindeer and run around the world in the middle of summer."

"Oh, I don't know," said Botto.

"It's obvious now," said Geimle. "We were planning on delivering those gifts you took *next* year. But there isn't going to be a next year is there. He wanted to make sure I understood it wasn't my fault. The plan wasn't ever going to work."

"Ho….ho….hold on," Motto stuttered. "What do you mean, there's not going to be a next year?"

Botto nearly sprayed hot chocolate all over the glossy table.

Geimle shrugged. "This is our last Christmas. The Big Guy's giving up. Maybe he's already given up. He thinks we can do this without him, but we can't. If he doesn't come back, we'll do what we can. If he does—and I still think he will—we'll make one last great ride, and then pack it in."

Malveno said, "You keep entering the vortex on some pretext of helping children—which isn't something we do, we're not that kind of elf—so we're guessing you're scouting out some place for us to go, some new Burzee? You wouldn't just do that on your own. No, and if he's sent all these elves away, they're probably all looking for Burzee."

"I think some of them probably just left," said Motto, but no one seemed to hear him.

"We've been kind of on cruise control for years anyway," said Malveno. "And then with the ice cap melting like it is…"

"I just thought we could still have a part in it," said Geimle.

"Well," Malveno stood up, "this is what I think. I think this is our last Christmas. But the Big Guy knows that. And he's going to come back before the twenty-fifth and we're going to go out with a bang."

46

CLAIRE WAS ACTING WEIRD. She'd been acting weird ever since she returned from California. It wasn't just that she was happy—smiling, tolerant, talkative—or even that she was present (she hadn't spent time in the basement since they got back)—the oddest thing was that she was failing to even notice things that should have driven her crazy. She hadn't made a fuss about the children coming back home (supposedly from a friend's house) so late. Just a few words about responsibility and "don't go doing that again" and that was it. She didn't comment on how unlikely it was that Jasmine and Tanya and Morris were somehow all at the same friend's house. Jasmine and Tanya had been convinced that only constant texting on the flight home in the sleigh—making one excuse after another, each one flimsier than the last—only this had prevented her from calling the imaginary friend's parents to make sure there was nothing funny going on or even charging over herself to drag the girls home by their hair and Morris with them. But now they didn't think she would even have noticed if they hadn't texted more than once or twice that whole time. Three times Tanya asked her what she was so happy about, and every time she responded by singing a snatch of a Christmas carol, which was usually whatever happened to be playing on Morris' dad's scratchy old turntable.

They knew it had something to do with Mark Tortare and California. But still, it was weird.

And what exactly did it mean? Did it mean she was staying, or did it mean she was going? The question never seemed to change, no matter what they did or said. Did it mean she was taking the girls? Or did it mean she was leaving them with Morris and his dad? It certainly meant she'd made up her mind one way or another and that she was happy with whatever she'd decided.

"I say she's staying," said Morris. "Just look at her."

"Maybe she got it out of her system," said Jasmine.

"I still think she's going," said Tanya. "This is one big final Christmas together. She never makes a big deal of Christmas. It's just a big good-bye party."

Jasmine said, "She does usually just put out a tree and that's about it for Christmas stuff."

Claire had gone into all the Christmas boxes in the house, hauling up from the basement things that had been packed away for years. Morris' dad had never been one to put a lot of effort into holidays. But some of Morris' stepmoms had filled the house with reindeer and candles and colored lights. And they always left the stuff behind. There was plenty of it. And Claire went out and bought more. She had the children outline the house and all the windows. And she put white lights on the bushes and knickknacks on all the shelves.

"But that guy was a bully," said Jasmine. "Can you imagine our mother putting up with someone like that? She must've seen it, and now she's decided she can't live with that."

"They'd kill each other," said Tanya.

"He was just protecting his property," said Morris. "And that was some nice house."

"That's true," said Jasmine. "She likes things like that. You really think she's going—with us or without us?"

Tanya grabbed a cardboard angel adorning the end table beside her, a cheap ornament with a slight bend in its halo. She crushed it. "I don't know."

"It's like she's never going to tell us."

"Like maybe we'll just wake up and find another one of those notes and she'll be gone for good."

"You can't let her do that," said Morris.

Claire peeked into the doorway to the den and called to the kids huddled together like a gang planning a heist, "What are you three up to? Come help me put the leaf in the table."

It was a big leaf, and it was an old table. You had to jiggle it a lot and pull pretty hard. But why would she want to expand the table? There was plenty of room for the five of them.

"In case we get any company for Christmas," she said.

"In case?" said Jasmine.

"Who's coming?" said Tanya.

Claire told Jasmine it would be nice if she'd bake some cookies.

"Who's coming," Tanya repeated in an angrier tone than she was accustomed to using with her mother.

Claire's humor fell away, "What's with that tone?"

"People don't just stop in for Christmas without being invited." Tanya waved her arms.

"What's in your hand?"

Tanya tightened her fist around the crumpled ornament. Claire grabbed her hand and pried it out.

"What'd you do to my angel?"

"I crushed it." Tanya sounded defiant.

"You crushed it? Well you know what happens now, don't you?"

"Maybe you could sing a song about it."

Claire slapped her. And everyone froze. The Christmas album on the ancient turn table crackled as it came to an end and the arm lifted. Tanya did not raise her hand to her stinging cheek. She looked out the window at the thin layer of snow on the back yard, then turned back to her mother. Claire was concentrating intently on the crushed angel, ironing it out with her palm as though it could be saved.

Tanya wanted to pull the ornament away and just tear it up. But she was too afraid to do that. Instead she said, "Is Tiara Williams coming?" She didn't even know why she said it or where it came from.

Jasmine gasped. Morris looked at Tanya in surprise. Claire stopped and looked up at her daughter, her expression blank. She may have been calculating how Tanya could have got into a locked drawer in a locked office. "How do you know about Tiara Williams?"

"Is she coming?"

"I suppose Willard told you. He said you contacted him. What did he tell you?"

"He told us it's none of our business," said Jasmine before Tanya could speak.

Claire clearly did not like that explanation. "Maybe," she said, "maybe she's coming. Maybe she isn't." She picked up the angel. "I'll deal with this later. Make the damn cookies."

And she went down to her office.

The three children stared at each other until they heard the sound of Claire's office door clicking shut.

Tanya pointed at Morris, "You make the cookies." Then she gestured to Jasmine and they tiptoed down the stairs.

Claire's voice came clear enough through the closed door.

"You didn't tell them?"

They didn't hear the reply.

"Well how'd they find that out?"

She must have had the volume really low, or maybe she had headphones on. They couldn't hear who she was talking to. But it had to have been Willard.

"Well they'll know soon enough, I guess."

Another pause and then, "Yes, of course I'm sure. Merry Christmas. What? Well get yourself a damn tree. That's not my fault is it? Goodbye."

Jasmine tried to pull Tanya back upstairs. But before Tanya could move, Claire opened the door.

"Did you want the gingerbread cookies, or the sugar cookies?" said Jasmine immediately.

Claire grabbed them both and pulled them into her office.

"What the hell is up with you two—listening in at doors. Didn't I bring you up better than that?"

"Who's Tiara Williams?" said Tanya.

Tanya recoiled as though her mother was going to slap her again. But Claire made no move in that direction. "Why you so fired up about Tiara Williams? I don't even know how you know that name. You tell me how you know that name."

Tanya shook her head. "You said we'll find out soon enough. Is that what you meant?"

"You sure know how to ruin a good day," said Claire.

"Is that what you meant?" Tanya repeated. "Who is she?"

At that moment, the doorbell rang upstairs.

"Well I guess it's about time to find out." Claire motioned them toward the door but they didn't move.

"We know you're leaving," said Jasmine. "We know you're going to go to California and move in with that Mark Tortare."

"What? Where'd you get…?"

"Jasmine thinks you're gonna leave us behind. I told her you weren't going to do that. But she doesn't believe me. Tell her you wouldn't do that."

Claire turned around. And suddenly she was fighting back tears. So was Jasmine. Tanya was already crying. Claire reached out to her girls and hugged them. She was going to say something, but it was obvious she couldn't do that and fight back her own tears at the same time. The doorbell rang again. Claire opened the door to her office and she grabbed Jasmine in one hand and Tanya in the other, and she pulled them upstairs.

Morris was in the living room staring up at a large man in a trench coat. It was Mark Tortare. He was looking down at Morris as though he was trying to place him. His two daughters were huddled behind him like a scene from *A Christmas Carol*. They lost their shyness when Claire entered the room. They ran over and gave her a hug.

"Now you take off your wet shoes before you go ruining the carpet," said their father.

Mark Tortare wiped his feet for emphasis and held out his arms to give Claire a hug. And then he noticed Jasmine and Tanya—and a very strange look came over his face. Tanya, and Jasmine, and Morris were absolutely baffled.

"Well that explains that," he said to himself.

Claire didn't seem to hear. She said, "Tanya, Jasmine, Morris, I want you to meet Mark. You can call him Uncle Mark. He's my brother."

Just then Morris' dad entered the room.

47

GULLNLE WAS HELPING KARBLE move the tables for the after-Christmas party. "Apparently," she said, "Claire was born Tiara Williams."

"Really?"

"That's what they said."

"How did we not figure that out?"

"They're all celebrating Christmas together," said Gullnle, "all the remaining Williamses—which are really the Tortares because apparently no one wanted to be called Williams any more after they were taken away and got new houses to live in."

"Hey, Karble!" Motto's voice rang from the front of the hall. He and Botto were arranging the plants on both sides of the stage from which the Big Guy was going to give his annual celebration speech that launched the big Sigh-of-Relief party, assuming he felt good enough this year. He'd looked pretty well rested on December twenty-third, the first time anyone had seen him all year, when he came back from his long vacation. But you never knew how much the trip would take out of him. Everyone was in quite a rush as there was never much time between closing that door on the vortex and opening it back up again and it had already been two hours outside the vortex since they'd left. A row of potted poinsettias about five feet tall and crowned all over with dense red leaves stood behind a row of smaller holly bushes between two enormous Burzee rose bushes that were at the peak of their beauty with fist-sized blooms, blood red, and dark green saw-toothed leaves. In front of the hollies was a row of smaller roses, some old, some young, some just about to drop their seeds. You couldn't tell one from another by looking.

"Hey, Motto," Karble yelled back. Motto ran over for a hug.

"So what's this speech about?" said Motto. "Botto says it's gonna be something big."

"Oh, it's about how Claus, Ltd. is going to start out-sourcing," said Gully.

But she was interrupted by Karble. "No, it's not."

"How would you know?"

"Do you know?" said Motto.

But Karble changed the subject. "Gully was just telling me about Claire and the kids."

"Oh, I know all about that," said Motto.

"You do?" said Gully. "How does everybody know stuff?"

"Morris," said Motto. "He said that Tiara and Mark were both taken from the house when they were little."

"It was a very unhappy house," said Karble.

"Really?"

"They never went back," said Motto. "They moved around to different families the whole time they were growing up. They changed their names. Tiara wasn't old enough to even remember that her name had been Williams. But Mark Tortare did. And he found his father after he became a lawyer and then, when his father was dying, he found his sister and tried to get his sister to meet him to say goodbye."

"But she didn't believe she was who they said she was," said Karble.

"Morris said she just didn't want to have anything to do with him."

"So that was really Claire's father that died?" said Gully.

"Yeah, but by the time she made up her mind to meet him, it was too late. She just made it in time for the funeral."

"Well, that's sad," said Gully.

"The whole thing is sad," said Karble.

"Yeah, but now they're a family again, Mark and Claire and the cousins. So it's not all sad."

"What about Jasmine?" said Gully.

"You'll never guess," said Karble.

"I'll bet she's really Willard Tremont's daughter."

Karble let the table they were holding drop. "You're just too clever." The sound of the falling table got the attention of Botto who was just placing a small Burzee Rose on the lectern.

"Hey," he yelled. "Where's my help?"

"It's all done," yelled Motto.

Botto huffed and trudged over to the others.

"What are you guys all going on about?"

"Jasmine's mother left Willard and the baby girl and went back to China," said Karble. "And Willard knew he couldn't raise a baby, so Claire took her."

"So we were worried for nothing?" said Gullnle.

"It took her a while to find a good husband, but Claire is probably the last person on earth who would abandon a child," said Karble.

"Well that's a relief, because I was thinking I was going to have to give that human a good stern talking-to," said Botto. And everyone chuckled.

"So now that Jasmine knows who her father is, I suppose they'll reconcile too," said Karble.

"Maybe," said Motto. "Remains to be seen."

"Anyway, they're all staying together now. And they're going to visit California in the spring."

Karble was about to ask whether Mark Tortare had told Claire about seeing the kids in California and whether he'd agreed to pay for the tickets, but just then Philona startled them all by clearing her throat.

"I don't suppose any of you see that gaggle of tables that still need moving or that banner that needs unfurling or those chairs that need unfolding? Let's save the socializing for the party or I know of a few openings in clown inventory."

"Why do we need so many chairs?" said Gullnle.

"Why do we need clown inventory?" said Botto.

Gullnle's question was answered when the vortex door opened. All the elves of the North Pole were standing by as usual to cheer the Big Guy back home. An invigorated Santa Claus waved to the crowd lining the route as the reindeer pulled his sleigh around to the back entrance to the hall. But what was astonishing was the great army of delivery elves who followed him out of the door— many many more, hundreds more, than had entered with him. It was not *all* the elves who'd left in the previous years, and it was probably not enough to fill all the empty jobs at the Pole, but it was apparent to everyone that many of those who gone off in search of Burzee were returning to the pole. They filled every chair the elves had set out for the speech and more. The Big Guy waved to all his helpers as he approached the lectern. Geimle and Malveno and a whole row of managers and supervisors took their places on the stage. The Big Guy took the microphone from the lectern and walked to the middle of the stage and bellowed a huge Santa Claus laugh.

"What a fabulous year," he ho-ho-hoed. And the speech that followed was the most inspiring that anyone could remember. The room was rapt as he told them all he'd been up to since last Christmas, how, with the help of Karble, he'd monitored closely the operations of Claus, Ltd. And how proud and how sad he'd been from what he'd learned. He'd wanted to get the pulse of the pole, he said. He'd watched so many elves leave and so many people turn Christmas upside down in the world below. And then he'd heard Geimle's speech to the West Wing, and he knew he had to make a decision. "Everything ends," he said. He'd always known that. "There is a time for everything, and maybe our time had run its course, and maybe it was time to frame the picture and make a toast. When time runs out, it runs out," he said. He'd been sending elves into the world and into the vortex as well for a long time already by then, some to find Burzee (which none had managed), some to find another place to go if Burzee was not found, maybe a place to move the operation or maybe a place to retire for good. *But there was no other place*. "If Claus Ltd. is going to survive, this is where we have to do it," he said. People were everywhere now. There was even a permanent place where people lived on the South Pole. And as it melted down there, more and more would come.

And then he told the story of Geimle's plan for saving Christmas. And everyone laughed. And then he told the story of Motto and Botto and Gullnle and Karble and the human children. And everyone cheered. "No, no," said Santa Claus, "this is the only place for us. And this is the only work for us to do. We have to be here to do our work. We just have to hope it lasts and work to make it last as long as it can. Our work is still good work. Everything ends. But this is not our time. What we do is music that still rings out in the world below; you can hear like a bell in a room of voices."

And then he called Malveno and Geimle to the center of the stage.

"And now a new Christmas tradition," said Santa, smiling broadly.

"The sleigh," said Geimle, smiling less broadly. And the door at the back of the hall opened and a colly-sleigh came in, driven by Haymin, pulled by Pacer and Fearless. It came to a stop at the front of the stage. Haymin climbed down and took his place on the stage.

"Botto, and Motto, and Karble, and Gullnle, please take your places," said Malveno. And the four elves climbed aboard. Then Geimle and Malveno climbed in and Santa took Haymin's place. And Santa Claus announced the first annual After-Christmas Parade, which would be conducted every year in honor of those elves whose outstanding feats did the most to keep Christmas alive.

"Once around the hall, then out the door and into the streets, then once around the pole into the sky."

"Every year?" said Botto, when they'd cleared the stage, waving to the crowd of cheering elves below.

"Who knows," said Santa.

Interset Press is a small, independent press located in Southern New Hampshire. Lacking deep pockets for promotion in the crowded, competitive field of commercial fiction, it relies on word-of-mouth advertising. If you enjoyed this book, please tell your friends, rate the title on Amazon.com, or put a comment on our Facebook page.

www.ingramcontent.com/pod-product-compliance
Lightning Source LLC
Chambersburg PA
CBHW050510260626
47157CB00004B/1263